Moon Window

Other books by Jane Louise Curry

ROBIN HOOD IN THE GREENWOOD
illustrated by Julie Downing
ROBIN HOOD AND HIS MERRY MEN
illustrated by John Lytle
THE CHRISTMAS KNIGHT
illustrated by DyAnne DiSalvo-Ryan
THE GREAT SMITH HOUSE HUSTLE
WHAT THE DICKENS!
THE BIG SMITH SNATCH
BACK IN THE BEFORETIME: TALES OF THE
CALIFORNIA INDIANS
illustrated by James Watts

Moon Window

by Jane Louise Curry

MARGARET K. MCELDERRY BOOKS

Margaret K. McElderry Books
An imprint of Simon & Schuster Children's Publishing Division
1230 Avenue of the Americas
New York, NY 10020
Book design by Michael Nelson
The text of this book was set in Deepdene.
Printed in the United States of America
First Edition
10 9 8 7 6 5 4 3 2 1
Library of Congress Cataloging-in-Publication Data
Curry, Jane Louise.
Moon window / Jane Louise Curry.—1st ed.
p.   cm.
Summary: While staying with her elderly relative at Winterbloom,
Jo tries to solve the mysteries that haunt this strange old house
situated in the midst of the New Hampshire woods.
ISBN 0-689-80945-X
[1. Haunted houses—Fiction. 2. New Hampshire—Fiction.
3. Mystery and detective stories.]
I. Title.
PZ7.C936mo   1996
[Fic]—dc20
95-52558
CIP
AC

For Gretchen

For Better or Worse

As the organ sang out the first trumpet notes of the wedding march, Mrs. Lucas slid a worried look at her granddaughter JoEllen Briggs. *Pum pum pah pum!* The congregation of Lucases, Briggses, Masseys, Mateers, and their friends rose to their feet and turned as the second, louder *PUM PUM PAH PUM!* rang out. All one hundred and thirty-eight faces beamed up the aisle with smiles. All, that is, but Jo's. Jo's pale face was blank under the band of silk rosebuds that nestled in her froth of dark red curls. She sat straight and still and studied her hands, neatly folded in her lap.

Mrs. Lucas sighed. Her daughter Liz Briggs, Jo's mother, was about to become Liz Massey. Five years earlier, Jo's father had died in a car crash on a snowy mountain road in Colorado. Since then, Jo had had Liz to herself. Everything had been Jo and Liz, Liz and Jo. This year, George Massey had come along, and Jo, to put it politely, had become "difficult." George couldn't be nicer, Mrs. Lucas thought, but, poor man! It was going to take more than good humor to get through the next few months with his new stepdaughter. At this moment, as he watched Liz start down the aisle, he wore an almost comical look of happiness. If only Jo would stop being the Wicked Fairy at the Feast!

"Joanna Ellen!" Mrs. Lucas whispered sharply. She gave her granddaughter's shoulder a light tap instead of the shake she felt like giving. A shrieking, kicking tantrum would almost be a relief after the angry silence Jo had kept for the past month, but now was not the time to provoke one.

Jo did not twitch at her grandmother's touch. She sat like stone. Mrs. Lucas gave a small, silent sigh, and turned to watch as Liz stepped down the aisle on Jo's grandfather's arm. She smiled. Both Liz and Mr. Lucas looked pleased and proud enough to be walking on clouds instead of carpet.

Jo would not look up from the hands clenched in her lap. She could not tell whether the painful knot in her chest was her heart or her stomach. She was desperate. There must be *some*thing she could do, or in a moment it would be too late. Her mother was only yards from the altar. If— if she fainted into the aisle, they would have to stop. They would have to call for a doctor, or the paramedics. She pressed her Adam's apple and tried to concentrate on feeling sick, but could not. Sometimes it worked, but not now. Her mind was too crowded with a jumble of angry and fearful thoughts. The day was a warm Saturday in early June, but she felt a pinprick of cold tremble deep inside, as if the temperature were fifteen degrees below zero and her heart had begun to freeze.

Father Wilson cleared his voice and began to speak. *"Dearly beloved, we are gathered together here in the sight of God . . ."*

Jo watched stonily. By turning her head slightly, she managed not to see George at all. She looked straight at and through her mother, not seeing the peach-colored silk suit, or the curly dark hair, loose and long, under the cream lace veil. Instead, she concentrated all the angry jumble of her fears and fierce resentments, directing them for once at her mother, rather than George.

At the altar, Liz Briggs swayed slightly, then caught herself as George reached out to steady her with a hand on her elbow. Jo, startled, dropped her eyes.

". . . If anyone can show just cause why they may not lawfully be joined together, let him now speak . . ."

Jo's fervent hopes died in the brief silence after the priest's question. No one leaped up to cry, "Stop the wedding! George Massey is married already and keeps his lunatic wife locked up in the attic of his house!" No one shouted out, "Stop! George Massey is really Hugo Bascomb, wanted by the Arizona police on charges of embezzlement!" It was hardly surprising. George might have wrecked Jo's perfect life, but everyone else adored him. He sang baritone in the church choir, where Liz, who sang alto, had met him. He was big, and good-looking. A law professor. A little bit dorky, but only a very little. Absentminded, too, and a little rumpled.

Jo, on the other hand, for as long as she could remember, had tried to be perfect. She had gone happily to Saturday piano lessons, French classes, and Gymnastics Club. She helped her photographer-mother with darkroom work. She sang alto in the youth choir at church, going to the Wednesday evening rehearsals with her mother. She had attended classes in cookery, clay sculpture, and computer graphics with her mother and, by furious concentration, became a whiz at whatever she tried. In her heart, Jo cared little for any of it, except the gymnastics, which she loved. On the balance beam or the uneven parallel bars she emptied her mind of her bone-deep fear of losing her mother, as she had lost her father. She had to. Up in the air, she had to love the work for itself. On the ground, she was too intent on keeping life "just so." Perhaps, she worried, that was one reason why her mother had come to love easygoing George better.

And now Jo's whole life was changing. The framed family photographs, as well as the green velvet sofa, old Briggs dining table, Siamese-drum coffee table, and the Oriental carpets from their apartment in Cambridge would be put into storage or sold. They had brought the beautiful worn sofa, the jewel-colored rugs, and all the rest with them from Colorado. Jo and her mother had lived in Cambridge for only a year and a half, but the furnishings themselves were "home." Now only their clothes and books and trinkets were to go to George's house in Boston. George's sofa was puffy and white, his dining table glass-topped. He had peach-colored curtains and sea-green carpets, all chosen by his stuck-up sister-in-law. Magazine-y. Unreal.

". . . and, forsaking all others, keep only unto him, as long as you both shall live?"

Afterward, on the front church steps, the two families joined the bride and groom for a group photograph. Jo stood, sad and unsmiling, between her mother and grandmother while the laughing crowd arranged itself around them. By the time everyone was in place, Jo had drifted back and sideways to stand behind her grandmother, out of the camera's view. Only Mrs. Lucas, watching from the corner of her eye, noticed.

"All right, everyone." The photographer raised a hand. "Ready? One . . . two . . ."

Just before the count of three, Mrs. Lucas sidestepped neatly into the space Jo had left, leaving Jo too surprised to frown at the camera or turn away.

Click!

"Here, dear," Mrs. Lucas said quickly. "Here's your little bag of birdseed." She tossed her own birdseed as the bride and groom, amid cheers, dashed for George's old gray Volvo.

Jo, with seeds flying all around, turned and threw hers, bag and all, at George's seven-year-old nephew and hit him smack in the eye.

A Change of Plans

Halfway through the wedding reception, Jo's grand-mother was frantic.

"Have you seen Henry Lucas?" she asked one of the guests. "The bride's father? Oh, there, I see him over by the band. Thank goodness! Excuse me . . ."

She made her way among the candlelit tables around the dance floor of the hotel's Regency Room. When she reached her husband, she leaned down to whisper in his ear. He rose and followed her out into the wide hallway.

"What was that about Jo?" he asked.

"We have to do something, and quickly. If Liz hears, she'll call off the honeymoon. You know she will."

"Calm down, Peggy. If Liz hears *what?*" Mr. Lucas

steered his wife toward two nearby armchairs and sat her down.

Mrs. Lucas drew a deep breath. "If she hears that Jo can't go to Holyoke. George's brother Lawrence has just told me that Jo can't stay with them for the next three weeks after all. His wife, Ann, has put her foot down. Both feet. Because of the boys. Apparently Jo has been a perfect *witch* all week to both those nice little boys. What are we going to do, Henry? I thought of packing her off to Cousin Cassie's, but Marjorie says Cassie and Jack and the children left St. Louis four days ago for a white-water rafting trip in Utah."

Jo's grandfather frowned. "Are you hinting that we ought to take Jo home with us to Colorado? Think again, Peggy. We have only two days at home before we take off for the Geological Society conference in Los Angeles. Why not summer camp for Jo? New England has to be full of summer camps."

"Ye-es." Mrs. Lucas was doubtful. "It is. But would she go? She's never been to camp. I don't think she's ever been away from home at all overnight except when she's been with us."

"At her age?" Mr. Lucas snorted. "But you're probably right. She does keep an eagle eye on her mother— fusses over Liz as if she were a china doll. Probably locks her up in the glass-fronted cupboard at night."

A Change of Plans

Mrs. Lucas sighed. "When she was small she was a sweet little thing. Now I catch myself looking at her and thinking of Witch Ellen. That's what Cassie and I called the old painting at Winterbloom of one of our ancestors. What about—" she began, and then her face lit up. "Granty! I was about Jo's age the year I visited Granty Nell at Winterbloom. Why couldn't—"

"Are you serious?" Jo's grandfather stared. "I thought your Great-Aunt Macallan was over a hundred years old."

"Yes, but she invited Jo's cousin LuAnn for a month last summer. The invitation came out of the blue, Susan said, and LuAnn had a wonderful time. Granty is a bit frail, but she still loves having children around. And she does have live-in help."

Mr. Lucas frowned. "I thought you said Winterbloom was a strange place. A dark old house. And isolated."

"Oh, that didn't matter. I liked it. Loved it. Besides, we're desperate. If Liz finds out that no one wants Jo, she'll make George call off the honeymoon." Mrs. Lucas looked up and down the broad hallway. "We need to find a telephone."

Into the Woods

Jo stood beside elderly Miss Macallan in the driveway of the old house called Winterbloom. Together
they watched the winking brake lights on Jo's grandparents' rental car as it crunched out the gravel drive
on its way back to Boston and the airport. The
Lucases, running late, had time only to unload Jo's
bicycle and two suitcases, exchange a few bits of family news with Granty, and give Jo a hug and a kiss
before they drove off in a spurt of gravel.

Jo was stunned. Her grandparents had actually
gone. They had dumped her in the middle of the wild
woods and were flying home to Colorado without
her. All the way up across Massachusetts and into
New Hampshire she had told herself that they would
not do it. Could not. Her mother might be able to cut

her love into pieces as if it were a custard pie, and give George half or more, but her gran and granddad could never love her any less. Never. She had told herself a dozen times along the way that they would change their minds and stop at the next service station to telephone for a third flight reservation to Denver.

It hadn't happened. Instead, Gran told stories of her first visit to Winterbloom. Of Hamish, Granty's shaggy sheepdog, who found her when she lost herself in the Winterbloom woods. Of Ailsa, the Winterbloom cook back then, who made cherry soup and "silk pudding," and even— a strange sort of joke— a blackbird pie with a real blackbird that flew out and away when the top was opened. And of the attic trunks full of silk gowns and lace gloves and fringed shawls for playing dress-up. Jo had listened for a while, and then pretended to doze off. It had not been her plan to fall asleep in earnest, but she slept all the way up Interstate 91 and did not wake until the middle of the bridge across the Connecticut River between Westminster and Walpole. She kept one eye open on the way through the town, but then dozed off again. Only when the car made a sudden sharp turn up into the private lane did she straighten up and pay attention. Granddad had almost missed seeing the Winterbloom sign, and swung the steering wheel sharply at the last minute.

Winterbloom. Jo turned to stare at the tall stone

house with its narrow windows, peaked roof, and corner tower. Atop a hill in the middle of the New Hampshire woods, it was as nonsensical a sight as a live dolphin in a garden fishpond. Miss Macallan— "Granty"— herself was surprising, a middling-tall, handsome old lady who wore an odd ankle-length brown jumper dress over a faded blue cotton blouse. She was thin and a little stooped, with a braided coronet of white hair, dark eyes, and a slender, high-bridged nose. The neck of her blouse, where a button was missing, was pinned with a silver thistle. Her long teardrop earrings and the heavy rings on her long, thin hands were silver too, and the bird-shaped handle on her cane. She had a nervous, eager manner that was oddly girlish. Gran had explained earlier that Granty wasn't really her great-aunt, but her grandmother's first cousin. That meant she was Gran's first cousin "twice removed," or first-cousin-two-generations-back. That meant that she was Jo's first cousin four times removed.

As if Jo cared. How *could* they go away and leave her? Well, she was not going to stay.

She had made her plan even before she packed for her three weeks' stay with George's brother's family, and after Gran had arranged the trip to Winterbloom, it had taken only a telephone call to the New England Bus Authority about bus times to make the plan fit Winterbloom. By tomorrow afternoon, she would be at home in the apartment in Cambridge. When her mother heard she had run away, she and George would be on the next plane. If for some reason Grandpa or the police couldn't reach them right away to let them know, the pantry cupboard at home held enough canned food to last for weeks. She could go out for milk or groceries at midmorning or afternoon, when everyone in the apartment building was at work. If the police came to look for her, she could take the darkroom key and lock herself in. The darkroom was air-conditioned and had a little refrigerator. Because of all the chemicals, the expensive photographic equipment, and the DARKROOM—KEEP OUT sign on the door, no one would be surprised that it was locked. The only other key was in France on her mother's key ring.

Her mother was never going to risk sending her away again.

"Come with me, JoEllen," old Miss Macallan said in her clear, unexpectedly strong voice. Over her shoulder she called, "Thomas! Mind you close and latch the gate."

Startled, Jo turned to see a gaunt, gray-haired figure in overalls, carrying a long-bladed grass scythe, step out from the shadow of an apple tree on the edge of the orchard and move to close the barred white gate. Then he paced stiffly back along the low stone wall with the long-handled scythe against his shoulder, almost as if it were a spear and he a sentry.

Curiosity gleamed for a moment through Jo's gloom. "Who's that?"

"That's Thomas Craig, my housekeeper's husband. He and their son, young Tom, look after the orchard and garden."

"Oh."

Miss Macallan peered down with a *Now-which-aunt-or-cousin-or-grandparent-is-it-that-you-remind-me-of?* frown at Jo's pale, sullen face beneath the dark red hair and its handsome French braid, as if it were a face that stirred some long-buried memory. Then she looked Jo up and down. The child was too thin. Miss Macallan took in the closely bitten fingernails and the tightly polite smile, too.

"I do hope you'll like Winterbloom as much as I shall enjoy having you," she said. "Having visitors is always like an old-fashioned spring tonic, without the nasty sulphur taste. My rusty old memory dusts itself off, and my wrists and knees forget to groan."

Jo's eyes would have dodged away, but Miss Macallan's dark, eager ones met and held them. The old lady smiled, almost shyly. "Do I call you 'JoEllen,' or have you a pet name?"

"Jo. Everyone but Gran calls me Jo."

"I like that. Jo." The old lady paused for a moment,

as if she were tasting the name. "And you must call me Granty. All the cousins do."

Jo met Granty's eyes for the first time. For one startled moment she had felt as if she were staring into a mirror at a wrinkled, white-haired self, but the illusion was no sooner seen than it was gone. Even so, she shivered.

Old Miss Macallan shivered, too— though it might have been one of the tremors of old age. "Well then, Jo, let us walk around to the terrace in back of the house. I believe Mrs. Craig has made us a cake. Since your gran and grandpa had to rush off, we'll have it to ourselves."

Granty walked slowly. She did not actually lean on the silver-headed stick she carried, but seemed to use it to make sure of her balance where the ground was uneven. Jo, with escape in mind, looked around carefully as she followed.

The house looked as if it had been set down in the New England woods by mistake— or wafted there by a crack-brained wizard. For one thing, most New England houses were made of wood, not stone. This one was not only built of stone, and oddly tall, but had a square tower at one front corner. All of the windows Jo could see were either small, or tall and narrow. Winterbloom clearly was very old. *And* damp, dark, and uncomfortable, Jo supposed sourly.

Moon Window

The house stood in the middle of a wide lawn of shaggy unmown grass. Rosebushes and beds of shrubs and flowers ringed the lawn. Beyond them stood Winterbloom's orchard of gnarled and knobbly old apple and cherry trees, a low stone wall, and then the wild winter hazel— "winterbloom"— trees that gave the house its name. At their backs rose the forest. In the middle of the wide lawn at the rear of the house, three huge, massive-trunked, thick-limbed elm trees towered taller than the house. The new leaves of the nearest elm cast a clear green shade across most of the raised stone terrace along the back of the house. Miss Macallan saw Jo look up at the giant trees, and smiled.

"Aren't they splendid? They're Scottish wych elms. Ellen Macallan Hawke, who built the house, had these three shipped as saplings from Scotland. A number of the old American elms on the property have died from Dutch elm disease, but so far these have been lucky. We pamper them."

Jo hardly heard. Her eye had wandered to the far end of the terrace where, high overhead, a turret— complete with pointed cap— perched at the corner of the steep roof. Below, at ground level, beyond the terrace doorway into the house, panes sparkled in two windows taller and wider that any of the others Jo had seen. Near the windows, four wicker chairs sat around a weather-beaten terrace table. The table was set for two, with a teapot, a cut-glass pitcher of what looked like lemonade, and a cake on a glass plate under a net cover.

"Ah!" Granty exclaimed. "Just the ticket. Mrs. Craig's lemon cake is the best there is. You will have a big slice, won't you, Jo?"

"Maybe a little one," Jo said.

She sounded as if she were only being polite, but that was hardly the truth. On the drive from Cambridge, Granddad had stopped near Westminster for lunch, but when he and Gran ordered seafood salads and freshly baked bread, Jo had said, with an air of brave suffering, "Nothing, thank you." Granddad had the waitress bring her a toasted English muffin, but she had eaten only half of it. Now she felt hungry enough to devour an entire cake.

"Sit anywhere you like, my dear."

Jo sat down stiffly in one of the wicker chairs beside the table. Granty poured a glass of lemonade and handed it to her.

"I take it you don't like your new father," she said unexpectedly. "While your grandma was telling me about the wedding, you looked as sour as a basket of green lemons."

"*Step*father," Jo corrected quickly. After a moment she added calmly, "Everyone else thinks he's the best thing since chocolate nut-crunch ice cream. I think he's a toad."

Moon Window

She slid a sideways glance at Granty. Instead of the disapproving frown she expected, she saw only a smiling old lady hovering like a nervous hawk over the lemon cake, cake knife poised. Her ringed hand shook a bit as she made the cuts, so that both slices came out quite large.

"Drat! Shall I cut this in half for you?"

Jo hesitated for barely a moment. "No, that's fine. Thank you."

Granty poured herself a cup of tea. "Oh, dear. Would you rather have had mint tea than the lemonade? I should have asked. As I recall, it was your mama who introduced me to mint tea. She spent a week here when she was— eleven, I believe. It was the last summer before she and your grandparents left Boston for Colorado, and I've not seen her since. But I expect you know all that. When she and Mr. Massey come on the twenty-sixth to collect you, I hope they can stay for a day or two. I would enjoy that."

The twenty-sixth. Two weeks of honeymoon in France and then another at home in Boston on their own. Moving things to George's home and the rest into storage. Jo had the sick swiftly-falling-elevator sensation she was almost used to by now. She knew exactly when she had felt it first: the Monday evening before their Valentine's Day trip to the White Mountains. She had been helping her mother in the darkroom, hanging up strips of developed film

18

to dry. Her mother had turned to her in the dim red light and said, "George has been dropping little hints about getting married. How would you feel if that happened?" Jo had pretended to misunderstand. "Why should I care if he gets married? Anyway, who would marry him?"

Now, when she tried to swallow, the bite of cake would not go down. It took three tries.

"Try a sip of tea." Granty's voice was vague, but as she passed a cup to Jo her look was as sharp and intent as if she were an entomologist looking at a strange new sort of caterpillar under a magnifying glass.

Jo sipped. The tea, hot and minty, helped. She stared into her cup, expecting more questions, but none came. When she did raise her head to look across the table, the old lady's eyes were half closed. Odd— with her head tipped back, Granty didn't seem to have any more wrinkles than Gran. Jo wondered how she could be over a hundred years old. She didn't have the used-up, dried-out look of the oldest old ladies in the nursing home Jo's school orchestra had once visited. Her face looked— blanker, somehow. Unlived-in. As her head tipped slowly forward, instead of slipping from a doze into sleep, she suddenly twitched awake. Jo, caught staring, hastily speared her last forkful of cake.

Granty's eyes crinkled into a rueful smile. "Dear me, I usually make it upstairs before I take my afternoon nap. And I did want to show you around the house first. Would you like to explore by yourself after you've had another bit of cake?"

Jo was startled halfway out of her I-insist-on-being-miserable mood. A chance to explore on her own was exactly what she wanted. Her mouth still full, she nodded her "yes."

"Good. And while you are at it, Jo, you must choose which bedroom you would like to have as your own. Meg Fraser, Mrs. Craig's Thursday helper, has made up the beds in the Green Bedroom, just off the second-floor landing, and in the Yellow Bedroom on the third floor, but there are six guest rooms in all. If you prefer one of the others, you mustn't feel shy about saying so."

"How will I know which rooms belong to you, and to Mr. and Mrs.— Craig?"

Granty seemed not to notice her shift from mumbles to a more businesslike tone. "Mine is the one off the little second-floor sitting room." She took up the cake knife. "The Craigs don't live 'in,'" she explained. "They have a cottage in the woods west of the house. Now, will you have a second helping of cake?"

Jo tried to look as if only politeness made her hold out her plate, but she had a flicker of suspicion that Granty wasn't fooled in the least. She would have to be careful.

Winterbloom House

Jo stood in the middle of the sitting room— Granty had called it "the Great Hall"— and looked around in amazement.

The curved arch of the ceiling made the Hall half again as high as any ordinary room. The walls below were paneled in dark wood, and the stone fireplace at the far end was large enough to stand up in. The great windows along the terrace side, with their panes of old, wavy handmade glass, and a long window seat below them, were set deep into walls at least four feet thick. The room might have been a set for an old movie, the sort in which ladies wore jewels in their hair and gowns stiff with embroidery, and men wore ruffs around their necks, and swords and velvet hats. Only the lamps and piano and bookcase, and the jigsaw-puzzle pieces spread out on one small table, were too modern to fit.

Granty settled herself on one of the two sofas that faced each other in front of the fireplace.

"Explore where you wish, dear. And if you find you do like one of the other bedrooms best, just pop your head into the kitchen and tell Mrs. Craig so. Jo?"

Jo had not heard. She was staring up at the life-sized painting in a heavy gold frame that hung on the wall opposite the windows. The long-ago lady who stood there with a great wolfhound at her side returned Jo's stare with a piercing gaze of her own. Her ivory-colored gown was embroidered with delicate leaves and berries and flowers. Over it she wore an open-fronted, sleeveless robe of dark blue bordered with gold, and a gold lace collar stood up like a fan behind her head. The pearl drops on her gold earrings were the size of pigeons' eggs, and the center stone of the brooch that fastened the long, looped-up strand of her pearl necklace to her bodice was a ruby even larger. It was not her finery Jo stared at, though. It was the dark red, crinkly hair, the strong eyebrows, and the piercing black eyes.

"The lady. Who is she?"

Granty's eyes were closed. For a moment she did not answer. Jo thought she must be asleep already, but then she spoke. "She is our seventeenth-century ancestor, Ellen Macallan, from the north of Scotland.

She was the granddaughter of an earl, and at the time that was painted, she was married to a Sir Alan Dewar. I believe I'm named after her. Ellens seem to run in our family."

"She doesn't look like four hundred years ago—except for the dress. She looks like Cousin Susan, only fiercer."

Granty sounded startled. "Fiercer?"

"Well, as if she wanted her own way. She must have been used to getting it, too. She looks as rich as anything."

Granty did not answer, and when Jo next looked, the old lady had dozed off.

In the gloomy front hallway, Jo crossed the flag-stone floor toward the front door. The two dark paintings of fruit and flowers in heavy frames, and the dark, knobbly-legged table and high-backed chairs along the paneled walls looked as if they must be as old as the house. The only window was a tiny one beside the front door. Jo reached out to try the large key in the front door's great iron lock. It turned easily enough, but noisily. The long iron bolts above it gave a loud groan and moved only a fraction of an inch when Jo tugged at them.

Jo gave a quick look over her shoulder toward what she guessed was the kitchen door at the back of the hall, but no Mrs. Craig appeared. If the front door were bolted shut at night, there would be no getting out that way, so Jo turned to the doorway on her left. Beyond it, she saw a heavy-legged dining table and chairs of a dark, polished wood on a worn green carpet. The chair backs were high and carved and the dark paneled wall opposite the fireplace was hung with old needlework scenes of ladies and gentlemen out riding and hawking and hunting deer. The two tall windows at the far end of the room were narrow: eight panes high and three wide. Their heavy green silk curtains were faded and the hems frayed, but even so they looked rich. Jo crossed to the window not blocked by a spare dining chair. Its sash stood open several inches at the bottom, but when she tried to raise it further, it refused to budge. With a shrug, she returned to the entry hall.

To the right of the front door, in the corner that from the outside of the house looked like a tower, a wide staircase with a heavy, carved banister stepped upward into gloom. Running upward with it along the wall was a modern stair elevator. Its seat rested above the bottom step. Jo climbed to a landing with a narrow arrow-slit of a window, then turned and climbed past another landing to reach the second floor. There, the door to the Green Bedroom across the hall landing stood open. She saw paneled walls painted a soft green, windows hung with faded green silk curtains, and a canopy bed with old draperies and bedspread embroidered with twining ivy vines. An iron Franklin stove stood in the fireplace in the end wall.

The next-door bedroom was smaller and L-shaped, but except that the curtains and bed hangings were a deep rose color, its furnishings were similar. Across the hall, next to the stairwell, the door of the sitting room Granty had mentioned stood open, too. Inside, next to a small writing desk, a grandfather clock stood sentinel beside a door into a bedroom. Jo could see through to the foot of a heavy oak canopy bed with bedposts carved with vines and grape leaves. The embroidered bed curtains were faded here, too. The carpet was shabby, and the wall opposite the front windows was hung with tapestries.

Jo frowned. Winterbloom House was a puzzle. If Granty were rich enough to own a huge house and have gardeners and a housekeeper and a housekeeper's helper, why couldn't she afford new curtains and carpets? Old things could be nice, but not when they were ratty. It didn't make sense.

The four bedrooms on the third floor were old-fashioned too, but more ordinarily so. They seemed larger, as well. Each, like those on the floor below, had a fireplace fitted with an iron stove, and a tall oak or cherry wood wardrobe instead of a clothes closet. In one room a small painting caught Jo's eye. It was a moonlit view of looming hills, all ghostly green and gray and violet. In another bedroom she was drawn to a queer old embroidery on the padded top of a stumpy-legged little stool. A ring of animals dressed like men and women danced from corner to corner on its dark blue background. When Jo caught herself smiling, she jammed her hands in her pockets and scowled. But she was drawn back down the hall to peer again at the little painting. A small, dark shadow in the misty valley below the hills appeared to be a house. It might even have been the twin of Winterbloom, but the mist made it impossible to be sure.

In the third bedroom, a small portrait in oils of a young woman in a tartan shawl and green silk dress hung over the fireplace mantel. Everything about the painting was stiff— the green dress, the girl's pose, her hair, her face— and yet she was queerly alive. Her hair was the same crinkly dark red and her eyes the same sharp black as those of the Ellen in the painting downstairs, and as Jo's own. The eyes appeared to follow her as she moved across the room, and as she turned back, the painted girl seemed to watch her with a shadow of a smile. The smile vanished as she reached the door. When Jo went back for a closer look, she saw that, like the eyes, the smile was an illusion. But this Ellen was— interesting. Jo almost liked her.

The room furthest from the staircase had a high bed with faded yellow brocade bed curtains and spread. The bed was so high that a carved oak step stool stood beside it so that the sleeper could climb onto it. Jo crossed the room to open the window and look down. It was a long way to the terrace below, with no rainspout to climb down, and no trellis with a nice, strong ivy vine. Looking up to the right, she saw that the base of the corner turret thrust up and out close overhead. Getting out of the house unseen was going to be more difficult that she had thought. The ancient elm tree at the corner of the terrace towered over the rooftop and thrust its great arms in all directions, but no sizable branch grew within reach.

Back in the hallway, Jo chewed at the corner of a fingernail. Which room?— not that she really cared, since it was only for one night. Undecided, she headed along the hall toward the stairway. Opposite the stairs she noticed for the first time a narrow door that had been painted the same off-white as the walls. Instead of a doorknob, it had a small pull-ring. Jo tugged at the ring, expecting to find a broom or linen cupboard, but instead, she saw a flight of steps climbing upward into shadow.

The attic of Winterbloom House was a huge, high-ceilinged space, where the corner tower above the main stairwell was walled off as a separate room and filled with old furniture and odds and ends. The main attic, dimly lit by a window at each end and a large dormer window on each side, was richly paneled, with a high, beamed ceiling, but like most attics, it held a jumble of objects judged too good to throw away and others that "might come in handy." The dusty floor was crowded with boxes, several old ironbound wooden trunks, and at least three canvas-covered brassbound ones. There were lampshades without lamps, too, and clothes racks hung with dusty garment bags. There were old-fashioned washbowls with matching pitchers, rusty old hurricane lanterns, fancy tabletop oil lamps with milk-glass globes, and orange crates full of dusty books. In one corner several pairs of ski poles and warped wooden skis leaned against the wall. Jo did not see the door at the far end, where the left-hand corner was closed off by a curved wall, until she ended up directly in front of it. Three broad, curved steps led up to a door. The door was ajar, and when she reached the top step it swung open at barely a touch. Inside, Jo found not another attic jumble, but an empty small, round, high-ceilinged room: the turret at the back corner of the house.

A hoop of blackened metal with holders for candles hung by a chain from the ceiling. There were two deep windows, little more than slits, and a large, round one between them. Late-afternoon sun poured in through the narrow window on the left, which faced west. The deep middle arch in the thick stone wall narrowed from four feet wide down to a circle perhaps two and a half feet across. Jo's heart gave a queer little jump when she saw the round window. The frame holding its panes was like a wheel, with a central circle and spokes radiating from it like rays from the sun. The panes were thick, and full of tiny bubbles that glinted like silver sparks. The elm leaves that brushed the window on the outer side sparkled like green garnets and pale emeralds.

"A moon window!" Jo breathed. That was what she had heard her mother call round windows.

The window ledge was low and deep enough to sit on but, further in, the slant of the niche's overhead arch made it an awkward perch. The window itself would not open. Jo pulled at its handle-bolt, but it was firmly stuck. Over the years the window had been painted fast, layer by layer, into its frame. When she touched the yellowed ivory paint, her fingers tingled.

It couldn't be stuck. It had to open. *Had* to.

Jo blinked as her heart thumped. "Don't be silly," she said aloud, but even as the words came out, she was looking around the room for something sharp. She fumbled in her pocket, but the key chain with her pocketknife on it was in her old jeans, at home.

Knife. Knife . . . Almost before the thought "desk drawer" popped into her head, Jo was hurrying out and down the narrow, winding stair on her way to the second floor and Granty's sitting room. There, in the middle drawer of the writing desk, with the pencils and pens, she found what she hoped for: a knife with a sharp, stubby blade. Back up in the turret room, she cut away as much paint as she could from the bolt and its socket and then, following the painted seam between window and frame, made a shallow, curving cut around the circle. She felt the thin blade slice all the way through, but when she gave the bolt a tug, the paint around the frame began to crack and chip, and the window still would not open. Where one large chip had broken off, bright coppery metal showed underneath and, on it, traces of a faint design. Jo scowled, and then after a moment began a shallow V-shaped cut to try to clear the paint from the seam more neatly.

That worked. A few chips flew off as Jo pushed the window partway open, but she was able to trim the edges of the window and the frame to look fairly neat. Backing off the ledge, she brushed the flakes and trimmings down its slope into her hand and dropped them in a neat little pile against the baseboard.

As soon as she had done it, she stared at the little pile in bewilderment. "Why on earth did I do that?" she asked aloud. "What if it was painted shut on purpose?"

And what if it was? a voice seemed to whisper in her ear. *That doesn't matter. Look.* And then she saw it. Only inches away, a great branch arched out over the corner of the terrace and down to the trunk of the ancient elm tree.

For a gymnast, it was as good as a stairway marked EXIT HERE.

The Best-Laid Plan

As Jo reached the foot of the attic stair, she met a faint aroma of roasting meat. Her watch read five minutes to six, and her suitcases were still in the downstairs hall. She hurried down the main stairway, and in three minutes was up again, breathless, with the larger of the two cases. When she pushed at the Yellow Bedroom's door, its hinges gave a loud *skreek!* and so she left it ajar. Setting the case atop the carved wooden chest, she unzipped it, snatched out a clean shirt and skirt, and dashed to the bathroom.

By suppertime the sun had dropped to the treetops. The corners of the dining room were full of shadows, but two silver candelabra stood in the center of the table. Jo caught her breath in surprise. With the long table, the tapestries on the walls, and the shimmer of candlelight, the room looked like the setting for a feast in a fairy tale. For a moment she forgot her sulky mood, and smiled. The linen and lace tablecloth had a pattern of thistles and acorns, and the knives and forks and spoons were of heavy silver with a design of oak leaves and acorns on their handles. The cut-glass water goblets sparkled like diamonds.

Once she and Granty were seated, Jo announced that she had chosen the Yellow Bedroom.

"Oh, good! Your grandmother stayed there, and I chose it when I first visited Winterbloom, too." Granty smiled, but as she looked at Jo she had the same faintly puzzled look she had worn at their first meeting.

Jo looked up from buttering a piece of warm, crusty bread. "Didn't you live here always?"

"Oh, no indeed. I was born in New York. I first visited Winterbloom and *my* Granty when I was ten. Then, when I was seventeen and here on another visit, my parents died in a flu epidemic. I stayed on here until that September when, as my father had wished, I left for Mount Holyoke College. Later, when I was twenty-three and teaching school, I received a letter from Granty's lawyer saying that she had willed Winterbloom and all of her money to me on condition that I live here and take her name, Macallan."

"Wow," Jo said. "But didn't you care about changing your name? What did it used to be?"

"Fettes. Ellen Fettes," Granty answered. "And yes, I did mind, but only a bit. I loved Winterbloom, you see."

Jo scowled. "I wish someone would give *me* a house. Then I wouldn't have to live in George's boring old brick pile. It's not so bad outside, but inside it's all glass and shiny wood and stainless steel— with really blah pictures on the walls."

Granty shook her head. "Be careful what you wish for in this world, Jo. Wishes can come back to haunt you. I loved Winterbloom from the day I saw it, but since the day I came back, I've never traveled much further than North Walpole. I have never seen Venice. Or Vienna. Or even Virginia, for that matter."

Jo shifted uncomfortably. She gave Granty a vague smile, and took another bite of bread so that she wouldn't have to say anything.

"Still, we must make an expedition or two while you're here," Granty said. "Just up the river, the old eighteenth-century fort in Charlestown has been rebuilt as what I understand is called a 'living history museum.' Perhaps later in the week you would like to see that."

"It sounds interesting," Jo said politely.

"There are some nice young people, neighbors, nearby, too—the Thirkells."

"Mm-m," Jo said.

Mrs. Craig came in with a tray of serving dishes, and when she vanished in the direction of the kitchen, Granty took up the carving knife. "Now, Jo, what are your 'druthers': a thick slice of meat loaf or a thin one?"

"In between, please." With an effort, Jo smiled. She tried her best to eat slowly, but it was not easy. The meat loaf was better than her grandmother's, and the tomato sauce spicier. There was asparagus, too, Jo's favorite, and crispy little potato cakes, and crunchy apple and walnut salad. All of her attention was on her plate, and she did not see that Granty from time to time watched her with a faint, puzzled frown. She asked for seconds, and knew it was going to be hard to stay miserable in a house where pictures on the wall smiled, where beds had stairs and curtains, and where Mrs. Craig was cook. Jo reminded herself sternly how perfect life at home had been before George. Unless she did something drastic, it never would be again. "Before George." The words had the ring of "Before the Hurricane" or "Before the Earthquake."

Dessert was homemade angel food cake and fresh strawberries.

Granty had no television, but Jo decided she didn't mind. Most TV was boring. At home in the evenings— Before George, that is— after Jo finished her homework, if she and her mother had no choir rehearsal or class to go to, and no darkroom work to do, they worked on the cookbook they were writing for children. On Mondays they helped cook or serve dinner for homeless families at Martha's Kitchen in Boston. Only on the evenings when her mother went out with friends or to a dinner party did Jo watch television. Trisha, the sitter, was a Harvard student who spent those evenings buried in her physics textbooks, and Jo usually watched old movies.

In the Great Hall after supper, Granty brought out a large leatherbound photo album. Jo expected to suffer in boredom until it was time to go upstairs, but found herself becoming interested. There were photographs of the young cousins who had visited Granty over the past forty or fifty years. Among them were snapshots of Jo's own grandmother and mother at ten or eleven, climbing the apple trees in the orchard, posing in the front doorway, and leaning out the same dining-room window. It was eerie, almost as if the two little girls had been there together.

"Aren't there any of you when you were young?" Jo asked.

Granty nodded as she closed the album. "Yes, and some older even than that, ones *my* Granty took. Two more books full. If you're really interested, I can bring them downstairs tomorrow."

Moon Window

Afterward, Granty went to sit at the small table where the jigsaw puzzle was laid out. The box lid showed a picture of a castle on a high hill. The label said it was a five-thousand-piece view of "The Towers of Carcassonne" in France.

Jo wandered over to the bookcase. Most of the books were old. The oldest had covers of worn brown leather, and queer titles like *The Kingis Quair* and *The Buke of the Howlat*. Running a finger along the shelves, Jo settled for a not-so-old book with a title almost as odd, *Five Children and It*. She curled up with it in an armchair and turned the pages slowly, pretending to read, while she went over her escape plans in her mind. Suddenly, just as she thought, "I must get up before five," she saw the words "I *must* wake up at five," where her finger rested on the page.

You get into bed at night, and lie down quite flat on your little back with your hands straight down by your sides. Then you say, "I must wake up at five" (or six, or seven, or eight, or nine, or whatever the time is that you want), and as you say it you push your chin down onto your chest and then bang your head back on the pillow. And you do this as many times as there are ones in the time you want to wake up at . . . Of course everything depends on your really wanting to get up at five (or six, or seven, or eight, or nine); if you don't really want to, it's all of no use . . .

Jo gave a silent snort. Silly baby stuff! You might as well believe in magic. She went back to turning pages.

At eight-thirty Granty stretched and hid a yawn behind her thin, ringed hands.

"It's time I went up to bed, my dear," she said. "I'm sure it's a bit early for you, though. Stay down and read, if you like. All of the doors and windows are locked. Mrs. Craig sees to that before she goes home, and I bolt the back door after her on my way upstairs. When you're ready to come up, you can turn off these lights. I leave the light on in the front hall."

"I'll come now," Jo said hastily. She had things to do upstairs, and had no wish to stay alone with the first Ellen Macallan staring down at her. She managed a yawn of her own. "I feel like I could sleep 'til lunchtime." It wasn't a lie. Even though she wasn't going to, she would have liked to.

The chair elevator climbed with a low hum, taking the turns smoothly, but its chair carried only the tray with Granty's "bedtime treat" of milk and sugared oatmeal. Granty climbed the stair steps slowly under her own steam. Over her shoulder she observed, "Mrs. Craig was to have young Tom take your little suitcase up. It's not in the hallway, so he must have."

Jo found it hard to climb at a creep. Impatience made her fidgety, but she tried to keep the fidgets out of her voice.

"I saw him go up with Mrs. Craig. Before dinner." Young Mr. Craig had turned out to be a shy, middle-aged version of his gardener-father.

On the second-floor landing, Granty reached out to a strip of moulding that ran from the top step to the ceiling, and turned a black knob set at shoulder height. The knob gave a sharp click and a light sprang on in the hallway ahead. A turn of a second knob switched off the light below.

"Those are weird light switches."

Granty smiled. "Just old-fashioned. There are switches like them up on the next landing," she went on to explain, "and down the hall beside your bedroom door. Do you mind going up alone? Or shall I come with you?"

"I don't mind," Jo said. She did, a bit. It was a strange old house and she was not always as sure of herself as she tried to appear.

"Leave the hall light on if you like," Granty said. "Good night, my dear."

When Jo turned the button switch beside her own door, the Yellow Bedroom sprang to life, picture-perfect, and she stopped in surprise. The golden light of the two table lamps made the room more welcoming than it had been by day. The faded bedspread had been replaced by a crisp, fresh one of crinkly white cotton, turned down ready for bedtime. Her small locked suitcase sat on the dark wooden chest. The large case, which she had left open, had been unpacked and stowed on the upper shelf of the open wardrobe. A pair of pajamas were laid out neatly on the bed with her cotton scuffs set out on the floor just below. The room almost seemed to say, *How could anyone run away from me?* Jo was not pleased. She did not want to feel welcome or comfortable. Worse even than the warm lamplight and the tempting bed was the small three-cornered stool embroidered with the ring of dancing animals that stood in front of the arm-chair. The small portrait of Ellen Macallan in her green silk dress and tartan shawl hung between the two windows, and the mysterious little painting of the house on the wall beside the door. All three.

The changes would hardly have been Mrs. Craig's idea. Granty had to be the mind reader. For a moment Jo was pleased, but then she took a deep breath and turned to the small suitcase. None of that made any difference; she had her plan. She crossed to the alcove to open the window at the top and close it at the bottom— her mother's old bedtime habit— and as she tugged at the stubborn lower sash, she imagined she heard the murmur of voices floating up from below. She leaned further out, to listen, but heard nothing.

Instead of putting on the pajamas, Jo changed into a pair of jeans and dark T-shirt and turned to the small suitcase. She opened it with a spin of the combination numbers, 7-2-3, and flipped the lid back. There were her alarm clock, the small key-ring flashlight, and her knapsack and fanny pack, packed and waiting. The knapsack held a collapsible umbrella, her favorite old sweater, a long, black rubber flashlight, and her hiking boots. Her diary was in the outer pocket, and a pair of scissors for cutting her hair short, if she weren't too cowardly to do it. The police wouldn't be looking for a boy in baggy jeans and a T-shirt.

The fanny pack was most important of all. Its zipped inner pocket held the thirty-two dollars saved from Christmas and birthday gifts and the fifteen dollars from her mother for three weeks' worth of weekly allowances. Add the twenty-dollar bill Granddad slipped into her hand when he thought Gran wasn't looking, and the ten Gran had tucked in her skirt pocket when *he* wasn't looking, she now had seventy-seven dollars. That should be more than enough. She set out clean socks and a pair of old, well-broken-in gym shoes. Everything was ready.

She checked her watch. 9:05. She frowned as she picked up her travel clock to set the alarm hand. Its shrill buzz might not carry to the floor below, but if Granty's sitting-room and bedroom doors were open and she a light sleeper . . . Still frowning, Jo set the alarm for four o'clock and placed the clock on the bedside table.

The Best-Laid Plan

She padded down the hall to the bathroom, and on her return undid her braid, combed out the curly tangles, turned out the lights, and climbed the two steps up into bed. The mattress was lumpy. Jo wriggled around until she found a comfortable spot, then curled up and lay still.

A moment later she reached out, turned off the alarm, and stretched out flat with her hands straight down by her sides. Out loud she announced, "I *must* wake up at four," pushed her chin down on her chest, then banged her head back on the pillow. By the time she had repeated the spell four times, she had forgotten to feel silly. She gave a sigh, curled up again, and fell asleep.

Through the Moon Window

Jo awoke as suddenly as if a bell had rung. Bright moonlight spilled across the bed through the open curtains. She sat up and reached over to tilt the face of her clock up to catch the moonshine. Four o'clock exactly. Amazing. People really *did* have clocks ticking away at the bottom of their brains. Jo threw the covers back and swung her legs over the side of the high bed.

She was as quick as she was quiet. She pulled on the socks and gym shoes, buckled on the fanny pack and pulled on a loose, long-sleeved shirt over it, then stuck the key-ring flashlight in her pocket. There was no time to do her hair in the French braid she liked. Instead, she pulled a comb through it, pulled it back to braid it into a single fat pigtail, and fastened it with two elastic hair bands. She could redo it on the bus. Or cut it off when she got to Keene. Or not.

It took only a moment to roll the comforter from the foot of the bed into a long sausage and stuff it under the covers. She gave it a poke here and there. It didn't make a very convincing curled-up sleeper, but anyone who took only a quick peek in at the door might be fooled.

"Rats!" Jo whispered. That meant she ought to close the door. Perhaps, if she did it slowly enough, it might not skreek. She patted her pocket to make sure the little key-ring flashlight was there, and picked up the knapsack.

The door inched shut with a long, low groan, and then a loud *snock!* Jo held her breath and listened. Nothing. She switched on the small pinprick of light and slipped down the hall, keeping close to the wall. She knew from Gran and Granddad Lucas's old house in Colorado that floorboards near a wall did not creak as much as those further out, worn by years of passing feet. Once in the attic, she had no need to worry about floorboards. Granty's room was too far below for creaks and groans to carry. Even so, Jo had to go carefully. There were no electric lights. The furniture, clothes racks, and old trunks made the room a maze, and her pocket flashlight's tiny beam did not reach far.

In the turret room, moonlight streamed through the

round window. Jo dropped the knapsack in the light and looked at her watch— 4:22. Then she knelt on the curved ledge to work the bolt loose and open the window.

Outside, Jo could see here and there through the branches of the great elm tree that the sky was already pale with more than moonlight. She picked up the knapsack and then eyed the window. What if she got stuck, like a cork in a bottle? Quickly she knelt to open the knapsack and carefully wrap the flashlight in the bulky sweater. Then she buckled the knapsack shut, leaned out, and dropped it four storeys to the terrace.

Then it was her turn. In the half-light, the nearest branch of the great elm tree looked more slender than it had by daylight, and further out. To Jo's nervous eye the tree looked almost as if it had pulled up roots and taken a step away from the house.

Coward! She took a deep breath, climbed into the window recess, and took a firm hold on the window frame. Then, ducking her head, she worked her left leg out and eased it down to feel for a foothold. Reaching her left hand out and up, she grasped a higher branch, steadied herself, and then lightly shifted her weight from the window ledge into the tree. With both hands clasped around the upper branch, she edged her way in toward the great tree trunk.

Through the Moon Window

Elms are not the best of trees for climbing. Their upper limbs often branch too steeply up and away from the trunk before spreading out, and the wych elm's bark is rough. Jo's progress was made even slower by the heavy roof of leaves that shut out the moonlight. After six or seven gradually slanting feet, her bough sloped down steeply, and even with her hold on the branch above, Jo almost lost her footing. Turning, she eased herself down to sit astride the limb, then worked her way down backward, thankful for the protection of her jeans. When she reached the crotch between the branch and the great trunk, the worst was past. From there she could step from one great bough down to the next, as if she were on a circular staircase with uneven and awkwardly high steps.

The lowest of the great boughs branched out and up at least eight feet from the ground, but a few feet along its length, a lighter branch arched downward. She grasped it, and swung herself down and then along it until her weight bowed it down and her toes touched the terrace stones. There she pulled off the knapsack and took out the hiking boots and flashlight. After changing from the gym shoes into the boots, she packed away the shoes, buckled the knapsack, shrugged it on again, and was ready. Her watch read 4:52.

She had left her bicycle leaning against the house, beside the front door. Moving quickly and quietly, she slipped around to the front. The long shadow of Winterbloom House fell across the drive and far garden, but her eyes had grown accustomed to the gloom and she did not need the flashlight. Besides, Granty's bedroom windows were just above. Jo remembered to keep to the dew-damp grass and away from the drive. Gravel was noisy.

The bicycle was not there.

Jo peered behind every bush and around the far corner, but it was nowhere in sight. She stood and thought for a moment. One of the Mr. Craigs might have put it in the garage. Must have.

There was no garage in sight, only a grassy track that led back through the orchard. Jo followed it until, in the shadows near the stone wall, she saw a shape the size of a large cabin. Moving carefully— it might be the Craigs' house— she drew closer, and saw that it was a small stone barn. The long back side was built into the orchard wall, but unlike the squared-off quarry rock wall, it was built of roughly shaped field and forest stone. Its windows were tiny, and the shingled roof was steep. At the near end on the side facing the orchard, Jo found a double barn door, newish-looking, and fastened with a heavy, old-fashioned padlock.

"Serves you right," Jo muttered. She had double-checked everything but the bicycle. She held up her wrist to catch the light. 5:10. She would have to walk the two miles. "Two miles or so," Granddad had called it. At least she could still be off the road before the alarm was raised. All she had to do in Walpole before the bus came was find out where on Route 12 it stopped. She made her way back out to the curve of the drive, and then along its grassy edge to the gate.

Jo had not expected the gate to be taller than she was, or so heavy. Once unbolted, it swung open of its own weight on massive iron hinges, but that weight made pulling it shut again hard work.

Beyond the gate and high stone wall, the young winterbloom trees lifted moon-silvered arms to the pale sky. At their backs, tall pines crowded close, as if they meant to push on past and press up against the wall. Jo had not realized how dark it would be beneath their eaves. Two steps into the gloom, she stumbled as a stone rolled under her foot.

"Great," she growled. "*Break* your ankle. Stupid stone." Looking back toward the moon-gray shadow house, she could see only the upper floors over the top of the gate. Granty was still safely asleep. There was no light from Mr. and Mrs. Craig's house either, wherever "a little way through the woods" was. No one was going to see the beam from her flashlight. She switched it on and hurried into the dark.

At first, as the lane bent down around the shoulder of a hill and then straightened, the woods seemed thick with a strange silence. Even Jo's own hurrying footsteps were oddly soft, but then she saw that the rutted way was carpeted with pine needles and needles ground down to dust by passing wheels. Like her eyes, Jo's ears grew sharper in the darkness. She heard small scurryings on the forest floor and a muffled, distant *hoo, hoohoo, hoo, hoo*. From somewhere to the left came a soft snort and a rustling of feet and branches as if some large animal had shuffled off in alarm.

"Oh, sure," she scoffed aloud. "'Wolves and lions and bears.'" She was startled at the loudness of her voice. "Probably a raccoon," she added firmly. Even so, her heart beat faster and a chant, oddly familiar, began to repeat itself in her head.

Wolves and lions and bears! Oh my!
Wolves and lions and bears! Oh my!
Wolves and lions and bears!

It was hard not to skip to the bounce of its rhythm. "Idiot!" she snapped, and strode on. There were no wolves outside of Yellowstone Park, and though there might be bears in Colorado— she would never have walked into the forest at night there— this was New England, and close to town. People had lived here for— how long?— three hundred years? The nearest bears must be a hundred or more miles further north, beyond the White Mountains.

Through the Moon Window

At the thought of the White Mountains, Jo scowled. On Valentine's Day weekend, George had taken Jo and her mother to the huge old Mount Washington Hotel in the White Mountains for a skiing weekend. It turned into Disaster Weekend when George took her mother out on a sleigh ride and proposed marriage. Jo shivered and broke into a trot. The flashlight's beam danced from the rutted lane into the darkness between the great pines and back, and flickered across fallen trees and rotting trunks. This very minute it was— what?— late morning in France. *George Massey, I hope you choke on a fish bone. I hope you get sunburnt to a crisp. I hope . . .*

But her anger faltered at the feeling that something, somehow, was very wrong. She stopped abruptly, suddenly unsure.

There was nothing. The pine forest had given way to great elms and beeches, but they were as still as before. Even so, as Jo took a few more steps, the sense of wrongness grew stronger. Like a cat before a thunderstorm, she was frightened, and did not know why. For a moment she wavered, but then she stepped out again along the dark track.

Curiouser and Curiouser

A faint light glimmered through the trees, perhaps a hundred yards ahead. Startled, Jo stopped and switched off the flashlight, and saw a yellow glow bounce gently across the lane and vanish: a walker on the main road, going toward town. She drew a deep breath and let it out in a sigh of relief. Then she switched on the flashlight and set off at an ordinary walk. By the time she reached the end of the Winterbloom lane, the glow was far ahead, but Jo felt more comfortable just from seeing it jiggle along. She aimed her own light down at her feet, so that no stray flicker across the trees would make the other walker turn to look back.

The road lay deep in shadow, but was not so dark as the narrow Winterbloom lane. Here the trees were pines again, giants that made her neck hurt as she tilted her head back to try to see their tops. They towered along the road's downhill course, but had been cleared far enough back from its sides so that here and there a swath of pearl-gray sky lightened the shadowy downward road. It was an eerily beautiful hour to be out and walking, but Jo saw only the gloom and listened only for footfalls. The uneasiness stayed with her.

At the foot of the long hill, a narrow bridge made of great squared beams and wide planking carried the road across a stony brook. Beyond the bridge, a half-finished split-rail fence followed the edge of a partly cleared field. The smell of cold wood ashes hung in the air, and in mid-field a thin thread of smoke still wavered up from the broad, blackened circle of a burnt-out bonfire. On the far side of the field great black tree stumps squatted in the shadows. Along the fence a row of uprooted stumps held their tangled roots toward the sky.

Somewhere ahead, a voice called and another answered.

Jo switched her light off again. She could not make out what the voices were saying, except for one call that might have been "Yes, Mama."

The trees were so tall and dark, the strip of sky above so narrow, that it was as if the road lay at the bottom of a deep canyon. It was almost too dim for Jo to be sure of her way, but she went on without the light and tried to make her footsteps too soft to hear. From the corner of the half-cleared field, where its fence turned at a right angle to the road and straggled up a narrow side lane, Jo could make out a barn and farmhouse between the field and forest. Yellow light shone in a downstairs window and smoke curled up from a chimney. Three shadowy figures were moving toward her down the lane, one of middling size and two smaller. Children.

Quickly, Jo crossed the road to clamber over a fallen tree and slip behind the trunk of a great pine. The voices were quite close.

"Ross Burt told me," a boy's voice said. "He says tonight they aim to go over to Keene to steal back the old cannon. I mean to go along."

"Papa won't let you," objected a second voice. It was a boy's, too, but younger. "They're all grown. You ain't even fifteen."

The third child, a small girl, piped up, "It's only a silly old lump of iron, anyway."

"But it belongs to *Walpole*," Jo heard as the cheerful quarrel faded away toward town, ordinary children having an everyday sort of argument. She peered around the tree trunk and saw only three perfectly ordinary gray shapes, two in baggy trousers and a small third in a skirt, hurrying away along the shadowy road, but the feeling of strangeness did not go away. It niggled at the back of her mind, and each time she tried to give it a name, it skittered away like a bead of mercury at the lightest touch.

Unexpectedly, the narrow road met and ended at a wider one. Which way to go? There was no sign, but fresh-looking footprints in the dust decided her on the right-hand way. A hundred yards further on, a crude signpost at a crossroads pointed two downhill ways to Walpole: straight on, or sharply left. The forest trees were so tall that Jo could not see from which direction the early morning sun was shining. Walpole and the Connecticut River valley were to the west, but she had no way of knowing which way west was. Uncertainly, she turned left.

After a short distance, the road dipped to angle over a rushing brook on another wooden bridge of squared beams and heavy planks. Once beyond it, where the trees closed in to make a dim, low-roofed tunnel, Jo slowed. Half a dozen yards into the shadows, she turned aside to rest against a tree trunk. Her legs had grown heavy, as though she were wading through honey, or a dream. She tried desperately to stir herself. It was almost six o'clock, and the first bus was at seven. With an effort, she pushed away from the tree.

She had not heard the horse that came jog-trotting down the road behind her and drummed across the heavy planking of the bridge. As she appeared in the roadway, the frightened horse reared up, staggered, and then tried to whirl away. Its rider struggled for control.

"Fool boy! What do you mean by jumping out of shadows like that?"

When the horse had stopped its nervous sideways dance, the man dismounted and bent to examine its knees.

"Curses on you if you've lamed him!" he snapped. "I've been up all night seeing two new Pickerings into the world, and don't care to walk the last mile into town. Half a score of dog bites and warts and snuffles and scalded hands will be lined up outside my door before I've had a bite of breakfast."

Jo stared at the man as he led his horse around in a tight circle, scowling at its legs. He wore a black, broad-brimmed, low-crowned hat, and a black suit with an oddly long-skirted coat. A black bag was tied to his saddle.

The man gave a snort and remounted. "He's not lame, but no thanks to you. Next time you hear a horse coming up on you, use the wits God gave you, my lad."

With that, he was off and away at a brisk canter. Jo scowled as she followed. "Lad"? He had taken her for a *boy*. Since when did country boys wear pigtails?

Not for a long while . . .

Jo shut her mind to that whisper, and hurried along

the dusty road, a short, straight-backed figure in dark tan jeans, blue shirt, brown leather boots, and a green pack upon her back.

Just as baffling to her as the "boy" was the horse. Who ever heard of a doctor going on house calls, let alone on a horse instead of by car? And those clothes? He looked as if he belonged in the historical fort and village Granty said was just up the river from Walpole: Old Fort Number— something. Maybe he worked there. Maybe he was playacting at being a doctor . . .

A mile further on, just when Jo decided that she had taken a wrong turning, the woods opened out ahead and a church steeple showed itself among the treetops. At the edge of a wide clearing a roadside sign announced TURNPIKE and, beyond it, a long pole as thick around as a stout young tree stretched across the road at chest height. Rigged on one end-post so that it could swing open like a gate, the pole barred the road from the wider one that climbed past it and on uphill.

Turnstile. The word came to her out of nowhere as she stared at the wooden barrier and the dusty turn-pike that swept past it. Like the Winterbloom lane and all the roads beyond it, the turnpike was unpaved, a dirt road with ruts filled in with crushed stone.

Numb with disbelief, Jo turned to look at the church on its grassy knoll. A large, plain two-storey wooden building, it was painted straw color, and had a handsome three-tiered steeple topped by a weather vane. Two men nailing shingles on the roof paused in their work to look at her. Two others, unloading bundles of shingles from a horse-drawn wagon, paid no attention. Jo's knees were trembling, but she walked around the barrier and along the turnpike to the crest of its long, downhill run to Walpole.

The road ran down between cleared fields and patches of woods, with a farmhouse here and there, to the south end of a village surely too small to be Walpole, and with fewer trees than the Walpole she had glimpsed from the car. Yet there beside it was the wide Connecticut River— except that Interstate 91 no longer swept up along the Vermont side, and the bridge across it was not steel, but wooden.

A wooden covered bridge.

Jo turned blindly and ran, full tilt, back the way she had come.

The gate stood open.

Sun gilded the treetops, but the shadow of the forest still lay across the young Winterbloom orchard and garden. The house, pale against the dark pines at its back, looked less real than ever, a dark-windowed castle in a dream.

Jo had to catch her breath before she was able to push the heavy gate shut behind her. She shoved hard to make sure that the latch bolt caught. When she reached the terrace, her heart still pounding, she shrugged off the knapsack and sat down to change back into her gym shoes. Her fingers shook as she tied the laces. She bundled the boots into the knapsack and shoved it out of sight behind a bush at the corner of the house. Tomorrow morning she would sneak it into the house.

Tomorrow morning she would think about it all. Not now.

Not now.

In the shadows under the elm tree furthest from the house, a cloaked shape stood and watched as Jo climbed toward the high, round window. When she vanished, it stepped from the shadows. Tall, dark-eyed, with dark red hair flecked with gray, it moved swiftly out across the grass.

"Come, Orm."

A large gray wolfhound padded to her side.

Together they crossed the terrace and entered the house.

A Discovery

Jo awoke to broad daylight. The clock on the bedside table read thirty-five minutes past nine. For a moment she could not remember where she was. When she did, she sat on the edge of the bed and tried to remember putting on pajamas and climbing into bed after her flight through the forest. Everything after was blurred by sleep.

Unless she had dreamed it all. Jo scrambled down and padded barefoot across the floor. She was almost afraid to look. Her fanny pack lay on the armchair, but the knapsack and its contents were gone from the small suitcase. As she closed the case she saw that her hands and arms were red with tree-bark scrapes. Her hair was a snaggly mess. She stared at herself in the dressing-table mirror.

A Discovery

Where had she been? *When* had she been? Could she have fallen out of the tree on her head and climbed back up in a daze to go back to sleep and dream about a New Hampshire before paved roads or cars or utility poles? And long, long Before George?

George! She had completely forgotten George, and now she had lost a day to him. He was going to have everything his way for twenty-four more hours. She could picture him on the beach, her mother rubbing sunblock on his back, or see him making eyes at her over seafood salads at lunch.

Jo gave the wooden chest a sharp kick.

"Ouch!"

She had forgotten she was barefoot, and had to hop back to sit on the bed steps and clutch her toes until the pain stopped. She dried her tears with her pajama shirttail. First a bath and clean clothes, she decided. Then breakfast, if it wasn't too late. Then find the missing bicycle. *And* be as sweet as peach pie all day. Smile. Ask questions about Winterbloom. Let Granty think she liked being stuck out here at the world's end.

On the landing, a freshly bathed Jo caught a whiff of the aroma of freshly brewed coffee. Downstairs, Granty was seated at the dining-room table, sipping at a large, breakfast-size cup.

"Granty?"

"Who—?" The old lady blinked. "Oh, good morn-ing, Jo my dear. I'm afraid I was woolgathering."

Jo frowned. "Wool— gathering?"

"Daydreaming." Granty cocked her head. "Is that an old-fashioned expression? I suppose it is."

Jo's eyes flicked to the bowl and plate at the place that had been hers at dinner the evening before.

"Ah yes, breakfast," Granty said briskly. "We help ourselves. Mrs. Craig doesn't come over 'til ten or so. The cereals are set out on the kitchen counter, and there are English muffins or bread for toasting, if you like. The honey and jam and orange juice are here."

Jo smiled again, but as she crossed the front hall toward the kitchen door, she sighed. At home her mother always had breakfast waiting for her. Or had, Until George. After George, Jo began to find her mother "woolgathering" in front of the kitchen cup-boards. There had been burnt toast, or no cereal left, or no milk in the refrigerator: signs of a world turning upside down.

After two bowls of frosted cereal, two English muffins with strawberry jam, and a tall glass of orange juice, Jo went out by the terrace door to join Granty in the garden. She watched as the old lady made her way along the flower border, carefully snip-ping off a shriveled rose here and there. She wore the same jumper dress and blouse as the day before, and a frayed Panama straw hat.

A Discovery

"There are only a few blooms out this early. They need another week or two," Granty said. "Beheading roses once they droop helps to keep the new blooms coming."

"I didn't know that," Jo said brightly. She peered over her shoulder to see whether her knapsack was safely out of sight, but the old elm tree blocked her view.

"Granty? D'you know where my bicycle is?"

"Didn't we leave it standing by the front door? I meant to speak to Tom Craig about putting it under cover, but I forgot. I don't suppose one morning's dew will have done it any harm."

"It's not there. I looked."

Granty set down her basket and, stiff from bending over the rosebushes, slowly straightened her shoulders and stretched out her arms.

"Then Thomas or Young Tom must have put it either in the storeroom or the garage. The storeroom is on the right, just inside the back door. The 'garage' is really the old barn. If you go through the orchard on the far side of the house, you won't miss it."

"I think I'll go see. Then I'll come help pick dead roses."

Granty gave Jo a curious look and then laughed, an old-lady cackle that had an odd gurgle of little-girl giggle to it, too. "No need to butter me up, my lass! Deadheading roses is for finicky gardeners and old crones. You go exploring on your 'velocipede,' as my Granty called bicycles when I was a girl."

Jo hesitated for a moment, then headed for the terrace. As she opened the door into the back hall, she gave a quick look toward the bush at the corner where the terrace met the house.

There was no bush.

For a moment Jo was too alarmed to breathe. Then she blinked furiously, but still could see no bush. Dazed, she closed the terrace door behind her and went to stare into the storeroom: no bicycle. On her return to the terrace, she slid a nervous glance toward the corner shaded by the elm tree.

It had not been her imagination. There really was no bush.

"I *did* dream it, then," Jo whispered. But then where was her knapsack? "And my bicycle?" she asked aloud.

"Did you say something, child?" Granty stood among the roses, watching her.

"The— the bike's not there," Jo said numbly. "Not in the storeroom. I'll go look in the barn."

As she passed beneath the great elm tree, she slowed for a closer look at the spot where the bush should have been. Only grass, good solid sod, grew there, right up to the stone wall. There was no sign at all of digging or replanting. Slowly, Jo made her way around to the front of the house. Could the bush have been a pile of brush? Could it have been a stack of brush that one of the Mr. Craigs had gathered up and wheelbarrowed away, knapsack and all? She couldn't ask them about it. How would she explain about having left it hidden out-of-doors in the first place?

She stopped suddenly.

Her bicycle was exactly where it should be. It stood propped beside the front door, where she had left it.

At half-past eleven, Granty came down from her morning nap and found a pale-looking Jo in the Great Hall, leafing halfheartedly through a Nancy Drew mystery so old that its brittle pages had turned a yellowish brown.

"Mercy, where did you root that out? It must be one your grandmother or one of her cousins left here fifty years or more ago."

Curious, Jo turned to the inside front cover. It was inscribed, in beautiful handwriting, *To Peggy on her Birthday, from Mummy and Daddy, May 21st, 1935.* "That's over sixty years ago! I didn't know Nancy Drew was that old."

Granty smiled. "I believe I read somewhere that they rewrite them every twenty-five or thirty years to keep her up-to-date, turning roadsters into sports cars and typewriters into computers, that sort of thing."

"It must be confusing for Nancy," Jo said darkly.

Granty did not seem to find that an odd remark. "Very," she said. "Oh— did you find your bicycle, dear?"

"Yes." Jo nodded. She didn't say where.

"Well, that's good. Now, about lunch today: I thought we might have a bite of lunch at The Homestead, and then drive on up to old Fort No. 4, the historical reconstruction in Charlestown. On the way, we can show you a bit of Walpole, and the library and suchlike, so that you can find your way around if ever you want to cycle into town." Granty's eyes twinkled. "It should be a grand bicycle ride, downhill most of the way, but you might want Young Tom to collect you in the car for the ride back up."

Jo smiled halfheartedly, but she did notice that Granty was looking as pretty as she was excited. Her cheeks were pink, and she wore a periwinkle-blue dress and had brought a blue straw sun hat downstairs with her.

At noon when young Mr. Craig pulled up at the front door in a long, shiny old black Packard automobile, Jo scooted across the backseat and Tom helped Granty in beside her. He gave the old lady an anxious look as she settled herself, but she answered with a sharp shake of her head. Jo, busy with her seat belt, did not notice.

As the big car passed out through the front gate, Jo's eyes widened, but then she smiled. The gate was a wide, single, wooden-barred gate, about waist high, and painted white. Of course. She should have remembered that from the day before. She had dreamed a double gate, high, heavy, and unpainted, but then dreams were like that. They scrambled real and imaginary images together into new worlds of their own. It was the same with the forest. "Woods" was a better word for the shady world of trees through which the car moved downward. Where the forest of her dream had been dense growths of towering pines and strewn with the rotting trunks of fallen giants, these tidy woods were— *woodsy,* and full of spring-green light.

Jo relaxed and sat back as the car turned out of the graveled lane onto the road— the two-lane, *paved* road. Only in a dream could she have imagined how rutted the lane was, and how narrow and dusty the road, without thinking it peculiar. Now she paid close attention to everything that swept by the car windows. Nothing was familiar. Except— except up a side lane to the right, where she glimpsed a farmhouse much like . . .

A moment later, they came to a crossroads and Granty leaned forward to tap Young Tom on the shoulder. "Let's take the long way 'round, and down Prospect Hill, for the view," she said.

Young Tom gave her a searching look in the rearview mirror, but he nodded and turned south.

Granty fell silent. They had not gone far before her

fingers began to fidget on the handle of her handbag. Several minutes later, when the old Packard turned right for the second time, the old lady was clutching the handle so tightly that her knuckles were white. Her eyes were closed.

Jo did not notice. Through the front window on Granty's side, she was staring at a frightening echo of her dream.

There was no church, but Prospect Hill Road, like the dusty turnpike of her dream, ran straight downhill past fields and woods and a scattering of farms and houses, to Walpole and the river. The hills and river were exactly the same, but a modern bridge spanned the broad Connecticut River where she had seen a covered wooden one. Now the interstate highway was where it should be, running north along the river on the Vermont side. Walpole Village, though much grown, was still not large, and to Jo's eyes, the greatest difference was that it had more trees than her dream-Walpole.

How could she have dreamed a landscape she had never seen?

"Miss?" Tom Craig spoke softly.

Startled, Jo met his eyes in the rearview mirror. He jerked his head in Granty's direction.

"Miss Mac— is she all right?"

Jo turned and saw that Granty was shivering. Her eyes were dark and anxious, her face pale.

A Discovery

"It's nothing." Granty took a deep breath. "Pure silliness. I don't believe I can look lunch in the face, though. Perhaps when we reach town we should drop you off at The Homestead for a nice lunch, and point out the way to the library. Then Young Tom can drive me home and come back later to collect you there." She fumbled in her handbag for her wallet. "Here, this ought to take care of—"

Jo was alarmed. "No, I don't want to if you can't come." She unfastened her seat belt and leaned forward to whisper to young Mr. Craig. "Shouldn't we go to the doctor's? Or the hospital?"

"She won't never hear of it," he answered shortly. "Best just to get her quick home." He had already stopped and backed into a driveway to turn. In a moment the car was speeding back uphill. "She'll perk up once we're back onto Chapnook Hill Road," he said quietly. "Always has before. If she doesn't, I can call the ambulance. I've got my cell phone," he explained. "Used to be a member of the Volunteer Fire Department down in Walpole before I moved out here to live with the folks. Phone saves a lot of time when there's a fire call."

At Winterbloom, Mr. Craig drew up in a spray of gravel at the front door and hurried around the car to open Granty's door. Already she looked much better.

"I'm all right. I feel fine now, Tom," she protested, but she allowed him to help her into the house.

Mrs. Craig stood with Jo in the front hall and watched them up the stairs. She sighed.

"I knew it. Same thing happens every time Miss Mac tries to go anywheres. 'Aggrophobia,' she calls it. Soon as she's home again, she's right as a trivet, except for being miserable at not having her day out. She'll be fine after she's had a bite to eat and a bit of a lie-down. You come along with me, Miss Jo. I'll do up a lunch tray for you to take up to her. By the time you're down again, I'll have yours on the table."

Lunch was cold asparagus soup with a corn bread Mrs. Craig called "Indian cake." There was green salad, too, and a strawberry summer pudding with whipped cream. Clearly Mrs. Craig had expected their return.

Jo had seconds of everything but salad, and closed her eyes in pleasure as she ate. Once she finished the pudding, though, uncomfortable thoughts came crowding back. How could Prospect Hill Road and a huge swatch of New Hampshire and Vermont echo a dream? Did a ghostly turnpike truly underlie the real road? Next to that confusing thought, the mystery of the missing knapsack was a welcome distraction.

Jo set out to solve it. She began by looking again in the storeroom. It was not there. Or in a pantry cupboard. Or the barn-garage. Or in any other place she could think to look. She found no other flashlight, either. She could get away without the bicycle, but not without some kind of a light.

In the attic, she poked around in a number of the boxes with no luck. The old hurricane lamps she had noticed earlier, if not broken, were useless without oil or whatever they needed for fuel.

She stood, angrily biting her lower lip and thinking. Without a light, she would need to start for town tomorrow half an hour or an hour later than her plan called for. *And.* And she had to stop imagining things about her dream escape even if it had felt eerily real.

As she passed the old trunks, Jo stopped to lift the lid of the nearest and found jumbled shawls and scarves and shoes, then a black velvet cloak with a beaded collar, and a blue suit with wide, padded shoulders and a nipped-in waist. There was a black wool bonnet, an odd black wool skirt that she decided was for riding sidesaddle, and a hooded cloak of green silk. The other trunks held a similar jumble. Then she came to a large, long wooden box, heavier and much older, with the initials E.H. carved on its front. It was bound with iron bands and studded with nails to make it stronger, and had long iron hinges that groaned as Jo lifted the lid. On top was a yellowed linen parcel fastened with two large, rusty safety pins. Jo could not resist. She unpinned it and folded back the linen.

Moon Window

A faint scent of lavender rose from the folds of the gown that lay inside. She had seen it before. Tissue paper plumped up its stiff silk sleeves, and a fan-shaped piece of cardboard supported the stand-up gold lace collar. Sleeves and gown alike were embroidered with hawthorn and rowan-tree leaves and flowers, and jewel-red berries. It was either the three-hundred-year-and-more-old gown the first Ellen Macallan wore for the painting in the Great Hall, or a perfect copy.

Jo touched a finger to a silky rowan leaf, and drew it back with a shiver of awe. As she did, she heard a quiet sigh of pleasure, and looked around in sudden fright. The attic was empty. "I guess it was me— I," she said aloud, reassuring herself. But she pinned the linen wrapping up again and quickly closed the box.

The last trunk held clothes, too. On top lay a plaid dress, long-sleeved, with a collar and cuffs of cream lace, two dozen or more tiny buttons down the front, and a moss-green velvet sash. The fabric, woven of soft grayish blues and greens like colors seen in a fog, felt like wool and silk. The dress was beautiful. Her errand forgotten, Jo lifted it out to hold it up against herself, and turned to a tall, cracked mirror that stood propped against the wall. The skirt reached almost to her ankles, but the dress looked exactly her size. She smiled to see herself— except for the tennis shoes and jeans bottoms— looking as if she had stepped out of an old storybook. She wondered what Granty would say.

The thought *Why not wear it down to dinner?* whispered at her ear.

The idea pleased her. She hung the dress over the open lid of the trunk and rummaged eagerly down through the other old-fashioned dresses and coats. Halfway down, she uncovered a stiff ivory-colored shoe, its leather only a little cracked, and a pair of white stockings that looked close to her own size. Perfect. She groped further down in search of the second shoe, but before her hand closed on it, it met a bundle loosely wrapped in paper. The odd, bulky shape had a familiar feel to its fabric. And a familiar-feeling buckled strap. She pulled it up and out.

It was her knapsack.

Old Times

When Jo looked more closely, she knew it couldn't be her own. Or— that it was and it wasn't. It did look like her knapsack, but as it might after being stored away for ninety or a hundred years. It was faded, and smelled as musty with age as the dresses under which it had lain hidden. Jo unfastened the rusty buckle and drew her breath in sharply. Baffled, she pulled out a flashlight, a sweater, and a pair of dusty hiking boots, wrapped in paper.

The boot leather was dry and cracked. A rotten lace snapped when she pulled at it. The sweater was moth-eaten. She pressed the button on the flashlight and nothing happened. A closer look showed that the black rubber case was hard and cracked. It took all her strength to unscrew the bottom, and when she did, a brown, gritty powder came off on her fingers. The batteries would not shake out, because they were corroded solid. Jo pulled the knapsack open wide and gingerly, as if she were putting her hand into a tiger's mouth, reached in to pull out a skirt and blouse with her own name stitched on yellowed tape inside the waistband and collar. She began to tremble.

Shivering, she spread the contents of the knapsack out on the floor as if they were the pieces of a jigsaw puzzle. There had to be an explanation. Had to be! It *was* her knapsack, so it definitely had *not* been in the attic for fifty or a hundred years. Had— had someone got the whole thing soaking wet and tried to dry it out in an oven? Even if that wasn't crazy, when had there been time? But what other explanation could there be?

Jo's mind scurried in circles. Maybe— maybe one of the Craigs was what George called a "worry bucket," always imagining the worst. If he decided a mysterious knapsack might be a bomb, he— or she— might have dunked it in a tub of water before looking inside, and afterward tried to bake it dry. But not in the Winterbloom kitchen. Baked boots and black rubber would have made an awful stink, and there hadn't been one. There was the Craigs' own kitchen, though. Jo scowled. The theory had one large hole in it. Wouldn't batteries explode in a hot oven? She half-remembered a warning she had seen on a battery package. Wouldn't anyone with half a brain have looked to see what was inside a knapsack before sticking it in an oven?

Jo sat cross-legged on the dusty attic floor to stare at the pieces of the puzzle. Her hands smoothed nervously at the crumpled paper in which someone had wrapped the boots. The sheets were so brittle with age that bits along the edges broke off at a touch. Jo turned one around and saw that it was from a newspaper. The only part of the masthead left read . . . *Ipole, New Hampshire* and *July 1809*. Her startled gaze slid down the sheet to a report headed PICKERING TWINS and a cold shiver trickled down her spine.

> *Our friend, Dr. Sparhawk, reports that a midnight excursion to the Pickering farm on Jennison Hill on the 30th of June to set Mr. Pickering's broken leg was crowned at dawn on the first of July with the raising of a tumbler (or two) to celebrate the early but happy delivery of twin boys, both in robust good health. Our felicitations to the Pickerings on their good fortune in the latter event, if not the former.*

Immediately below was a paragraph that made her catch her breath.

> ### HEROIC RAID
> *At break of day on the fourth of July, to the accompaniment of applause and the ringing of the bell,*

with a triumphant cavalcade of about thirty young men as escort, the wagon bearing the Walpole Cannon back from its two-year sequestration in Keene rolled down Prospect Hill and onto Main Street. The crowd assembled along the way had heard the good news from the first outriders, who reported the dangers, labours, and success of the raid, and the courage of the raiders. A large party of the citizens of Keene pursued our brave boys, but took the wrong road . . .

A doctor and twins? The Walpole cannon . . . Keene . . . In *1809.*

If it was true—

Terrified, Jo scrambled to her feet. Suddenly the warm, stuffy attic was more than she could bear. Stumbling over lampshades and cartons, she made her way to the turret room to open the window for a breath of fresh air.

At first it appeared that the round window had been closed off. Light fell through the two tall slits of windows, but the deep, round recess between them was full of shadow. Jo leaned in to see what was shutting out the light, but her fingers met only the knob end of the bolt handle. When she bent close to see whether a branch might have fallen and wedged its leafy weight against the window, what she seemed to see *was* darkness: the darkness of a dim landscape at dusk, under a rising, full moon.

Before her mind could take in what her eyes had seen, Jo's hand had pulled the stiff bolt free and pushed the window outward.

Dusk?

And no tree.

Beyond the window lay no tree, no forest, no June afternoon. Instead, a full moon rose in a blue-gray sky and two bright stars winked high overhead. Rock mountain walls, rounded like giant hummocks heaped together, loomed high on either side of the house. The house itself appeared to stand on a hillock ringed by a deep ditch with a stone wall crowning its inner rim. Below and to the right, Jo could hear the rush of a stream running among rocks in its long fall down the valley toward the silver scrap of sea at its far end. Strangest of all were the sheer, shifting curtains of light, of pale blue and green, that shimmered eerily across the evening sky.

Jo squeezed her eyes tight shut, as if it were a spell and that would break it. When she opened them, nothing was changed. Reaching out and across to grasp the bottom of the window, she pulled it around so that the bolt knob was in reach, tugged it shut, and turned and ran.

Sitting in the bathtub half an hour before dinner, Jo shivered again and slid down until the water touched her chin. No matter what she tried to think of— of taking a glorious shower instead of having to clean out a bathtub after a bath, or making a perfect 10 on the uneven parallel bars, or even of George kissing her mother behind the ear— her mind kept turning back to the strange and darkening valley and the magical light show in its sky. *Weird.*

Abruptly, she pushed with her feet against the end of the tub and sat up straight. Once, at Cousin Susan's hilltop house near Fitchburg, she had seen pale, wispy ribbons of light in the northern sky. The Northern Lights. *That* was what the eerie light show had been. The aurora borealis.

But it was the stark, shadowed valley that bothered her most . . . And then she remembered why. Those same humped hills shadowed the valley in the little painting that hung beside her bedroom door.

The sooner she was gone from Winterbloom House, the better.

A Meeting

Granty was standing by the long oak buffet when Jo
tiptoed across the hall toward the dining room.

"*Oh!*"

A small silver tray clattered to the floor as the old
lady turned and saw a pale, dark-eyed child in a plaid
silk dress, white silk stockings, and ribbon-tied party
shoes standing in the doorway. Jo's hair, curly from
the steamy warmth of the bathroom, was a dark red
cloud gathered back into a bushy tail.

Granty stood staring, and then sat down abruptly
on the nearest chair. "Bless me!" she said faintly as Jo
knelt to pick up the tray and salt and pepper shakers
it had held. "Bless me!" she repeated.

"I'm sorry." A red-cheeked Jo found the top to
the saltcellar and scrambled to her feet. "Are you

A Meeting

O.K.? Honestly, I didn't mean to surprise you *that* much."

"No, no," Granty protested. She took a deep breath and then shook her head firmly. "It's all right. But dear me, how strange. How very strange . . ." She twisted the rings on her fingers.

"I thought I must be dreaming," she said. "That is my dress. For a moment I thought I was looking in a mirror— as if ninety-odd years were brushed away and I were looking at myself in a mirror. Very unsettling."

"I really am sorry," Jo said anxiously.

"Come, child, no need to look as if the sky has fallen. I'm perfectly all right." Granty drew herself up. "Go out to the kitchen, if you will, and ask Mrs. Craig to give you a dustpan and brush. Salt can't be good for carpets."

As Jo hurried from the room, Granty looked after her with a puzzled frown. Then, with a shake of her head, she reached into her pocket for a matchbox, to light the candles. Her fingers shook so, she dropped the first match and left a small brown scorch on the old lace tablecloth.

After dinner, Granty produced one of the photo albums she had spoken of, which she kept in her sitting room upstairs. The date **1900** was stamped in gold on the cover, and its oldest photographs showed Granty as a bright-eyed high-school girl in a high-necked white blouse, with a large bow tying back the hair that fell almost to her waist. Granty and her parents and various cousins appeared in scenes of a storybook-looking New York with horse-drawn carriages among the motorcars. Later came a serious-looking young college woman with her hair piled atop her head and a topknot shaped like a bun. The photos were interesting, but as Jo turned the pages and Granty explained who was who, Jo could think of nothing but the turret window.

Granty shook her head and looked at her watch as she closed the album. "Only eight o'clock!" She sighed. "I know it's a waste of a lovely long evening to go to bed so early, but I seem to be more tired than usual. I suppose that, if you don't enjoy entertaining yourself, we might be able to rent a television set and— what is it called?— a VCR?— and some films for as long as you're here. Without cable, I'm told the regular television picture would be very poor."

"No, no—" Jo said hastily. "There's lots to do. I love to read, and— and read. I'll be fine." And she could be up in the attic all the earlier.

"Well then, good night, my dear." Granty bent to kiss her cheek.

"Good night, Granty."

Jo stood in the doorway of the Great Hall to watch Granty cross the hallway and go up the tower staircase, and then took a deep breath. She was beginning to fear that the window's eerie valley to the sea might have been a daydream spun out of an old memory, a warm, stuffy attic, and the haunting little painting. But if she *hadn't* daydreamed it, and her morning journey had been real, what else could the window be but—

Jo's mind shied away from naming it.

Supposing . . . just supposing there were a way to open the turret window on to time— on to any time she chose. Why couldn't she pick a time just Before George? Why couldn't she go back nine months and send a letter to her back-then self in Cambridge: *Don't let Mother join the church choir, or she will meet a DREADFUL man there, and marry him.* Jo smiled and gave a snort at the thought, but her heart seemed to miss a beat and jump to catch up. Her mind whirred. Would she *believe* a letter out of the blue, even when it was in her own handwriting?

She might— if it told her something no one else in the world could know, she might. It was certainly worth thinking about. She was sure she could come up with something. She listened for the whiny hum of the stair elevator carrying Granty's bedtime snack to stop, and then waited a few minutes more before she turned off the lights in the Great Hall and went out to the stairs.

When Jo stopped in the Yellow Bedroom to change into her gym shoes, she was in too great a hurry to exchange the plaid dress for jeans. It would be all right if she were careful, she told herself. After all, she was only going to look. When she reached the main attic, the garden below its windows was still bright with the luminous green of an early summer evening. She switched off her pocket flashlight and stepped into the turret room, her heart beating loudly in her ears.

Once again, the circle of the middle window was dark.

Jo stepped closer, took a deep breath, hitched up the plaid skirt, and tucked its front up under the wide sash so that she could climb onto the sill more easily.

Through the glass, she could dimly make out a nighttime garden, lit by a full moon in a cloudy sky.

She tugged the stiff bolt open and pushed the window outward.

Outside, snow fell, and there was music.

Fat snowflakes drifted down to cluster in the grass and melt on the terrace stones. Moonlight shone through a break in the clouds and light streamed out across the terrace from the Great Hall. The tinkle of a piano floated faintly upward and, with it, dimly, voices singing.

Jo crouched in the window opening, her last doubt gone. Every strangeness in the dawn dream world she had fled through came crowding back: the bicycle that was gone and then not gone, the two gates, the bush and knapsack that were there and not there, the rutted track that should have been a graveled lane, and the little village still recognizable in a world of paved roads and utility poles. She had awakened into today, but 1809 had been waiting in the moonlit dawn outside the round window. The moon window that always opened on a full moon.

"Time," she whispered. "You're a window in time."

The tune that tinkled below was familiar. The voices were singing "Happy Birthday."

Fearful, but too curious to draw back, Jo inched out further, until she could look directly down. The bare elm branch that thrust out toward the window appeared heavier than it had been at dawn. Where it crowded against the house, it had bent and grown off to one side, so that it rubbed against the stone a short step below the window. The sturdy branch was as good as an invitation to the party.

Jo wavered between caution and a desperate curiosity. Caution edged her backward out of the deep window recess, but once she had stretched her stiff elbows and knees, curiosity drew her in again. *Whose birthday? And when? What harm can it do to look?* came the whisper in her mind's ear.

She was halfway down the tree before she realized that she still wore the plaid dress. It was too late to do anything but be careful not to snag it and to tuck more of the skirt up under the sash. Besides, its long sleeves helped a little against the cold. Looking down, Jo could see the grand piano just inside the great windows of the Hall and and the little gathering around it. Three were young— two girls of her own age or a bit younger, and a boy of perhaps eight— but the angle of her view hid their faces. She could hear laughter and voices, but not what the voices said. The skirt of her dress had begun to come adrift from the sash, but she managed to reach a comfortable perch on the next branch down before it pulled free.

The Hall was bright, lit by candles and by oil lamps with white glass globes decorated with painted roses. Jo watched as the plump woman at the piano struck up a waltz and a side-whiskered gentleman in a tailcoat and striped waistcoat and a small, pink-cheeked woman in a gray taffeta gown and white lace collar stepped out to whisk merrily around the room. Two gentlemen in black wearing high, stiff collars stood off to one side and watched. An old woman, gaunt and white-haired, with the fierce, dark-browed gaze of an eagle, sat in a high-backed armchair nearby. A thin woman in black and a crisp white apron hovered in the background.

The taller of the two girls came to sit on the end of the piano bench to watch the plump lady's playing and turn the pages of her music. When the waltz was finished and the breathless dancers swirled to a stop, she turned toward the window. Jo could not see the girl's face clearly because the light was at her back, but could tell, when she suddenly straightened, that her glance in the direction of the great elm had become a stare.

Jo looked down at herself quickly. She was well out of the light that spilled across the terrace, but had forgotten the moon that shone through the thinning clouds. *You're imagining me,* she whispered fiercely in her mind. *I'm a ghost and you're imagining me.*

The girl stood and came to kneel on the window seat, peering out. Jo froze like a rabbit that thinks the fox will not see it if it does not move, but she felt the searching eyes touch and hold her own. In the Great Hall, only the fierce old woman in the high-backed chair seemed to notice. She rose and made her way past the dancers as they twirled off to the hearty bounce of a polka. Her face, too, fell into shadow as she moved past the lamp atop the piano, but Jo was aware of the touch of her sharp eyes as clearly as if a hand had rested on her own. She felt the hair on her arms and at the nape of her neck stir and stiffen, as if she truly were a rabbit, and had blundered into a foxes' den.

The old lady only reached out a thin hand to touch the girl's chin and turn her gaze away from the window. As they turned toward each other and the lamplight, the girl began to speak excitedly. The old lady shook her head and smiled, and laid a finger across the girl's lips. The girl fell silent.

That smile, as dazzling as sudden sunshine, made Jo's heart ache and her bones feel weak as sand. Confused and oddly jealous, she watched as the girl, with a sheepish little nod, slipped down from the window seat and returned to the piano bench.

Inching down as slowly as she could, Jo eased herself onto the branch below so that she could see still more of the room. The warmth indoors was beginning to fog the windowpanes. She saw the woman who appeared to be the maid or housekeeper enter with a large silver coffeepot and pass among the guests, refilling cups. The stocky man with bushy side whiskers shook his head. Followed by the plump lady from the piano, he went to speak to the alarming old woman, and bow over her hand. The plump lady made an awkward half-curtsy, and then they were gone. The two girls moved to the piano and sat down side by side to play a four-handed round that ended in giggles and a tangle of fingers. The boy stood beside the great fireplace, jabbing at the logs with the poker to make the sparks fly.

Come on! What year is it? What year? Jo thought fiercely, as if, by thinking hard enough, she could will someone inside to step up to the window and trace the date in the moisture on a windowpane.

A Meeting

Their clothing gave her no clue that she could read. The dresses, and the men's coats, looked somehow more old-fashioned than those in Granty's photo album, but she could not say how or by how much. She wished she had paid more attention to the illustrations in her school history books. When did women's long skirts stick out just a bit, not a lot? She pressed her hands against her eyes and tried to remember: did the ladies in Abraham Lincoln's time wear bustles to make their skirts stand out in back? Or did bustles come later?

If only, Jo thought, she had used her head. She could have slipped in at the front door before people started leaving, and found an easier clue: a newspaper on a hall table, or a postmarked, dated envelope on the upstairs desk. *And then*— the thought made her heart beat faster— *why not? Why not take a quick look out the attic window?* There must be a pattern, a reason why it opened first on this time, then on that. For all she knew, climbing out through the moon window *from* the past might land you in the distant future.

"Sss-t!"

Jo sprang up like a jack-in-the-box and almost lost her balance. She looked around wildly. The guests had vanished. The Great Hall was empty, though the fire still burned on the hearth and one lamp still glowed.

The hiss had come from behind and below. There,

in the dark shadow of the great elm's trunk, stood the girl who had knelt on the window seat to stare out at the night-shrouded tree.

Jo quickly hitched up her skirt to stuff it under the wide ribbon belt again, and scrambled upward. The rough bark caught at her lace wristbands and scraped her legs, but she was too alarmed to care.

"No! Please!" The eager whisper followed her. "Come down. I won't tell. I promise I won't."

Jo stopped to peer downward. "You won't tell what?"

The girl sounded surprised. "Why, that you've stolen the birthday dress Mama and Papa bought me, of course."

Jo climbed down until she could make out the pale, upturned face. "Who— who are you?" she whispered.

"I'm Ellen Fettes. You may call me Nell."

Blow Out the Candle and Come

Jo felt lightheaded. She closed her eyes and rested her forehead against the tree trunk's rough bark.

"What was your name before?" she had asked.

"Fettes. Ellen Fettes," Granty had answered.

Jo drew a deep breath, then swung down to a bough on the shadowed back side of the elm, and dropped to the snow-wet grass.

The girl who stood facing her was a little younger, a little shorter, but still eerily like herself, with the same red hair and dark eyebrows. They could have been sisters, or certainly cousins.

"Oh, my new dress!" Nell Fettes wailed softly. "It's all schmutzy— and the lace!"

"No, it's all right," Jo said anxiously. She tried to

hush her. "Your dress is fine. This one's not really—it's not yours."

"Of course 'tis," Nell whispered loudly. "Mama packed the parcel in my valise, and I opened it up first thing this morning. Mama had Mam'zelle Michel make it up from the plaid I liked so much at Gilmores' shop."

"Then if that was your birthday party in there, why didn't you wear it tonight?"

"Because." Nell gave a twirl to show off a dark green dress with a yoke and sash embroidered with a design of maple leaves in rust and red and green. "Because Granty gave me this one, and I didn't like to hurt her feelings. It's a copy of one in *Godey's Magazine*."

"Look—" Jo thought quickly. "Your birthday dress is right where you left it. Go look. I'll even come with you. Just tell me what year it is."

1897! In the light of the candle Nell carried, the house looked little different from the Winterbloom Jo knew, but that only made it seem eerier. The two girls crept up past the second floor where the voices of Nell's Granty and the housekeeper could be heard, to the Yellow Bedroom. It, too, was the same, except that the only painting on the wall was a small still-life of peony blooms.

Jo nodded at the open wardrobe. "There. You see?"

Nell stared at the dress in the wardrobe. Beside its

fresh colors and crisp linen lace, the rumpled dress Jo wore was only a faded, dusty echo.

Nell was bewildered, but she apologized nicely. "I'm very sorry I called you a thief, but if you're not, why were you hiding up Granty's tree? Who are you? Where did you come from?"

"I'm Jo— Joanna," Jo said, truthfully enough. "From Cambridge."

Nell held up the candlestick to give Jo a searching look, from the twigs and dead leaves in her hair to her stocking feet. "There were no footprints in the snow," she announced accusingly. "I think that's very odd, don't you? If you don't tell me how you came to be up Granty's tree, I believe I shall have to tell her about you after all. You're one of the cousins, aren't you?" She watched Jo mistrustfully.

Jo hesitated. How else was she going to get up to the attic? *And what would be the harm?* asked a whisper in her mind's ear. "I could show you how I did it," she said after a moment, "if you climb down the elm tree with me."

Nell stared. "*Down?* Don't you mean 'up'? Besides, I don't climb trees. My knees go wibbly-wobbly in high places."

"Even just looking down? Even if someone's holding you?"

"I think so." Nell was bewildered. "What are you talking about?"

Jo considered. "Will they miss you downstairs?"

"No-o. The only one still there is Mr. Twiselton, Granty's lawyer from Boston. They'll think I went to bed."

"Then first we ought to put on old clothes, if you can lend me some," Jo said. "I've nearly spoiled my dress already."

"All right— I 'spose." Nell went to pull shirt-waists from a drawer, and fetch two dark skirts from the wardrobe.

When they had changed, Jo said, "All right. Now blow out the candle and come." She rescued the little flashlight from the pocket of the plaid dress, and switched it on.

Nell stared at the light, wide-eyed. "What is *that?*"

Jo almost dropped it. "A pocket electric light," she said nervously. "You've seen electric lights, haven't you? Mr.— Edison's invention?" She crossed the fingers of one hand behind her back, hoping that Mr. Edison *had* invented the electric light by now.

Nell nodded in awe. "Of course. Papa had our house in New York electrified last year, so we have an electrical light in every room. But— a lamp that you can put in your pocket— how wonderful!"

She blew out the candle and followed Jo.

The turret room, to Jo's surprise, was not empty. The floor was covered with a rich Persian rug, and the black iron chandelier held candles. To the right, books covered a long oaken table with heavy carved legs that was made to fit the curve of the wall. An armchair with a high, carved back sat nearby. Jo recognized the stool at its foot, the same triangle-topped stool embroidered with dancing animals that sat in her own bedroom. The portrait of the girl in the green dress hung on the left-hand wall, and the little painting of the castle in the misty valley was propped on the table, against a stack of books.

Nell climbed awkwardly onto the deep, slanted sill of the moon window, and pressed her forehead against the glass. "I can't see anything at all. Do you promise you'll hold my legs if I open it?" she asked doubtfully.

"Promise." Jo knelt by the window's sill. "Is it painted shut?"

"No." Nell's voice was muffled. "I undid the bolt. The window jiggles when I push, but it won't open."

"Let me try."

Something clearly was blocking it. "Probably a branch," Jo muttered as she took a turn at pushing. On her second shove, the window gave way suddenly, opening with a loud crash, a tinkling of glass, and what made no sense at all— an excited yapping close at hand.

"You've broken it!" Nell exclaimed.

"No," Jo answered slowly. But she did not move.

After a moment Nell saw her begin to crawl forward until, impossibly, she appeared to be on her hands and knees in thin air. Soon only the scuffed soles of her tennis shoes were visible, and then they vanished too.

"Oh, oh, oh!" Nell wailed. She clapped her hands over her mouth.

Jo's voice floated back. "It's O.K. Come look."

Nell shut her eyes and climbed, trembling, onto the sill. "Hold on!" she quavered. "Hold on. I'm coming. Here, take my hand. *Eeek!*"

She squealed as something cold and damp brushed against her hand, but then a warm, furry body wriggled up against her excitedly, and her eyes flew open.

A puppy!

She found herself looking into a long, shadowy room. The only light was from one small window and the roof's gable ends, which were open at the top. The room was long, but not wide. Its walls were of stone, its wooden beams and rafters squared and heavy. Wooden boxes and several large trunks and barrels were stacked along one wall. Beyond them, a curtain sagged across the end of the room. At the opposite end, a shoulder-high stone partition closed off what appeared to be a barn stall. In front of Nell, a wooden panel lay flat, and beside it a broken bottle and a patch of wetness on the earthen floor. Two pudgy, large-pawed puppies sat and watched her expectantly.

"Oh!" Nell said faintly. She looked behind her anxiously, and saw only darkness. Alarmed, she scrambled forward and stood up unsteadily. When she turned around to look behind her, she saw a lidless wooden box propped against the wall, and in it the moon window standing open from a frame that framed only darkness.

"Jo?" she whispered.

Jo had moved across to peer at the wooden boxes.

A smaller box, containing square nails and heavy iron hinges, stood open on the floor. She found a folded paper under the hinges that proved to be a bill of sale from a Mr. Aaron Burt in Northfield, Massachusetts. It was dated *12th October, 1764*.

"What is this place?" Nell quavered.

"I don't know." Jo put the paper back. "Except that it's before Winterbloom. It's wherever the moon window was in 1764 or so."

Nell stared at the darkness framed by the window. "Are you saying that— that it's tonight in there and one hundred and thirty years ago out here?" She turned to Jo, her dark eyes wide. "Are we really back in time? We are, aren't we? You were climbing *down* Granty's tree. You came out through the window from some other time and climbed down. But why come out through our window? Why not go back the way you came?"

"I want to know how it all works," Jo said. She peered behind the curtain and saw a low bed, a wide stone fireplace, a woman's clothing hanging on pegs on one wall, and a familiar-looking Persian rug hanging on the other. "I guess it always works in the same time direction— backward. The trouble is, you never know when in the past you'll end up. It jumps around. But there must be a reason," she muttered. "There must be a way to make it take you to the time you want . . ."

She broke off as she found herself in front of the largest of the wooden boxes against the back wall. Stained and battered and at least five feet long, it was bound with iron bands and bore the carved initials *E.H.* Of the traces of an old shipping address on its side, she could make out only *Naumkeag* and . . . *chusetts.*

"Look!" Jo hissed. "This is the same box that's in the attic at Winterbloom." She lifted the heavy lid with an effort, and peered inside. On top of the parcels inside lay a long roll wrapped in a material that looked something like old-fashioned oilcloth. "I'll bet you that's the big picture of Witch Ellen."

"What do you mean?" Nell asked nervously as she came to look. "The big portrait is hanging in the Great Hall. Oh!"

"What? What is it?" Jo lifted the lid as high as she could.

"The insides of the box." Nell reached in excitedly to touch the place where a portion of the hard, black material lining the box had been broken away. "The pitch. It was used to make ships watertight. My Granty says that's how Ellen Macallan brought her jewels out of England and kept them safe: she coated them in wax and wrapped them in silk and pasted them to the insides of her cargo box. Then she coated the insides all over with a thick layer of pitch, as if it were waterproofing. Most of the jewels must still be in here."

"Umph!" Jo let the heavy lid down with as little noise as she could. "Maybe she has to sell them all to build Winterbloom House." She took a frowning look around the odd room, and shivered. "It's late. We'd better go back."

Nell was not listening. Hugging a squirming puppy, she had wandered down the room, past the curtain and back again, marveling at everything. When she stopped to look out the window at the spring-green forest beyond the muddy clearing, she suddenly put down the puppy, and reached out a hand to touch a crude letter *M* carved deep into the stone sill.

"Joanna! I know where we are! This is Granty's barn. The roof looks different, but the stone part is the same. And this—" She pointed to the mark on the sill. "I've seen this there. It's the same."

Jo came to look. "If you say so. But, come on— we ought to go back."

"Go? Oh, no! How can we?" Nell cried. She clapped her hands. "Don't you see? It's spring out there— spring in *1764!* We can't go away without taking at least a peek. Just think! George Washington, is out there somewhere— in Virginia, I suppose, but *out there*. And Thomas Jefferson."

Jo wavered, then followed her toward the door. "All right. Maybe just a look."

". . . and Benjamin Franklin," Nell finished as she opened the door a crack.

In the next moment, she was leaning against it with all her strength, trying to close it, while Jo struggled to drop the heavy wooden bar into the iron brackets.

"And there was the French and Indian War," Nell added breathlessly as her shoes slithered on the earthen floor. "I forget the dates— but I— think it might— still be on!"

On the other side of the door, a tall young Indian gave a sharp crow of laughter and a mighty shove that sent both girls sprawling.

The Wise Woman

It was over in a moment. The heavy door crashed open, and almost before either of the girls could believe that what was happening was happening, they were being dragged by their wrists across a wide clearing in the forest toward the men tending the great bonfire that burned in its middle. The two pups ran after them, yapping, and nipping at their skirts and the Indian's leggings until he shouted and cuffed them away with his foot.

"Weel, now! What's this ye've brought us, Joshark? Twa lassies?"

The men throwing tree limbs and trimmings onto the fire were hard-faced, shabby fellows and, unlike the half dozen Indians who crowded close in curiosity, they stopped only for a moment to look, and then

turned back to their work. The one who spoke, a tall-
ish, stocky, red-haired, red-bearded man, looked more
curious— and irritated— than angry.

"Come, man! They didna fall from the sky, did
they?"

The Indian called Joshark shrugged. "Perhaps. I
found them in the wise woman's house."

"Did you now?" The sandy red eyebrows shot up,
and then bent down in a frown. Jo met the man's hard,
blue-eyed stare, but Nell, flustered, looked away and
then down at her shoes.

"Here, have you not looked at them, friend Joshark?
They're near as like as two peas in a pod, and the spit
and image of Ellen Hawke. You, lassie: what's your
name?"

"Joanna Smith," Jo said quickly. "And she's Nell—
Nelson. We're cousins."

Nell was frightened, but as aquiver with excite-
ment as the pups were. She looked up shyly. "Who're
you?"

"Who am I? Why, I am James Russell, master stonemason, summoned over the sea from Scotland by your
auntie or cousin, or whatever Mistress Hawke may be
to ye, to build her a fine stone house in the middle of
this wilderness." He waved his arm at the circling
trees, and glared at the girls, though he did not seem
really angry. "It's a magician she should have sent for.
Jamie Russell doesna ken how to build a stone house

withoot stone, for there's naught but big pebbles here-
about, and he's no factor, to be overseeing tree felling
and uprooting and the like, all to earn a smile from a
sonsie woman. She's a madwoman, your Ellen Hawke.
Ye're welcome to tell her I said so."

Jo stared at him. Russell . . . Russell. Her gran's name
before she married Grandpa Lucas was Russell. What
if Jamie Russell was going to be her great-great— her
five-or-six "greats" grandfather? She trembled as Nell
nodded, wide-eyed, and said, "Yes, sir."

Jamie Russell frowned, but there was a hint of
laughter in the blue eyes. "'Yes, sir,' is it? Since ye're
so agreeable, then answer me. How the de'il did you
come to be in the hoose? I shut the dogs in there
myself, not half an hour past." He looked straight at
Jo. "And none of your lies. 'Joanna Smith' and 'Nell
Nelson,' indeed!"

"We climbed in through the window at the back,"
Jo said nervously. It was true enough. Before she could
think of a reason or excuse he might believe, Nell
chimed in.

"We've never seen real Indians before," Nell said.
She looked from Joshark to his companions, half in
doubt, half in delight.

"'Indians'? What name is that?" Joshark shook his
head. "We are Abenaki, the 'men of the east.' The wise
woman is our friend. You have no need to fear us."

James Russell nodded. "That's truth. Mrs. Hawke

buys the furs they trap and herbs the womenfolk gather, and sells them to traders downriver."

"Today we bring the young wintersnap— 'winterbloom'?— trees the wise woman asks for," Joshark said, "and she will bring us iron tomahawks and pots."

"Where is she now?" Nell asked eagerly.

The stonemason shrugged. "Somewhere betwixt here and Fort Dummer. By now, I trust, this side of Walpole."

Jo caught Nell's eye. "We'll go wait in the house," she said.

"Indeed, ye'll not," James Russell objected. "Ye'll turn around and go back to the settlement by the road ye came. Ye'll be safe enough, and if ye meet Mad Ellen, she can play nursemaid if she likes. I've work to do, and no mind to be bothered wi' bairns, and a shocking pair of liars to boot."

"Oh, please, Joanna," Nell tugged at Jo's sleeve. "Do let us go. There is so much to see. But where *is* the road, Mr. Russell? I'm all turned around."

"I will show you," Joshark said.

Jo groaned. "I thought he'd never go back. And how did you learn Indian talk? What was he saying to you?"

"Indian?" Nell covered her mouth and giggled. "It was French. He said he thought you were *une petite menteuse superieur.*"

"And what's that?" Jo asked suspiciously.

The Wise Woman

"A splendid liar." Nell's eyes danced. "Well, you are! You tell lies by telling the truth. Or by not answering. Like not telling me your proper name, or 'when' you come from, so I keep forgetting you're not here-and-now ordinary."

"Right now neither of us is here-and-now ordinary," Jo said grimly. She snatched at Nell's hand to pull her from the muddy track in among the drooping branches of a hemlock tree. "Look, don't you understand how really, really dangerous it is for us to be here? Gran's— my grandmother's name was Russell before she married Grandpa. What if this Ellen Hawke is supposed to marry Jamie Russell and be my five-or-six 'greats' grandmother? And what if we accidentally do something that— that— I don't know, maybe something that keeps him from staying here?" She drew a deep breath. "I saw a movie once where one of the characters went into the past, and because he was in the park talking to the girl who was going to be his mother just when the man who was going to be his father walked past, it meant his mother and father never met, so the man began to fade, and finally just went *poof!* He didn't exist anymore. Don't you see? He hadn't known she was his mother. His going-to-be mother, I mean."

"What's a 'movie'?" Nell looked at Jo blankly, and then cocked her head to one side. "You're truly fibbing now, aren't you?"

Jo didn't answer. Standing in the silvery hemlock shade, in her imagination she saw herself sitting beside George and her mother on a sofa, with a chubby baby on her lap. The baby gave a happy smile and a gurgle, and then went *poof!*

"You *are* fibbing, aren't you?" Nell asked anxiously.

"Yes," Jo said, after a moment. "I mean, I made up the story about the man. But it's still true. And we're going to cut straight up through the woods and climb in the back window of the barn for real. Right now."

Holding tightly to Nell's wrist, she ducked out from under the drooping fringe of branches, and clambered over a mossy fallen tree. The forest was so dense and its green shadows so deep, that instead of climbing in a straight line toward the hilltop clearing, they struck out parallel to the road. The way there was brighter, for where trees had been felled to widen the track, light shimmered through gaps in the leafy roof.

Nell suddenly pulled back. "Did you hear that?"

"What?" Jo froze for a moment. "I don't hear anything." She made as if to move on, and then stopped. It was horses Nell had heard. Both girls crouched down out of sight.

The sound came closer only at a *clip-clop* pace, but ahead of it loped two large salt-and-pepper gray dogs, muddy-legged, running single file. Then the first horse climbed into view, head bobbing, the large pack on his back swaying a little with each step. The second horse, too, wore a pack saddle laden with a wooden box on each side and a fat bundle on top wrapped in canvas and tied fast with rope. Puzzled, Jo and Nell half stood to peer through the tangled brush that screened them. They saw a third packhorse following, and that none of the three was fastened to another by so much as a piece of string.

The fourth horse carried a rider, a tall woman who rode with the reins looped around her saddle horn. She might have been asleep for all the attention she paid the road. She wore a blueberry-colored dress with the skirt slit back and front so that it hung down the horse's sides, and under it dark green breeches and knee-high boots. Her hair was hidden by a plain blue bonnet tied, Pilgrim-fashion, under her chin, but her shawl was a bright scarlet red. In that green wilderness, the shawl was like a shout in the silence.

"Do you think it's she?" Nell whispered.

"Who else?" Jo answered shortly.

The horses passed within eight or ten yards. As the rider drew level with the girls' hiding place, there was no mistaking the dark family eyes and strong eyebrows, the reddish wisp of hair that escaped the bonnet, and the long, straight nose. She had to be Mr. Russell's Ellen Hawke. Her face was not exactly young, but not yet middle-aged, and as she passed, her head was tilted back and eyes tightly closed, as if by listening she could hear every footfall in the forest, from the bear's paw to the foot of the beetle under the jack pine's bark. Jo stopped breathing. Nell covered her mouth with both hands, but her eyes shone.

A moment later, the four horses slowed together to a stop, and the dogs came circling back. Ellen Hawke leaned forward to stroke her mount's neck, and in a voice as clear and bright as silver, called out into the stillness. "'Tisn't neighborly, you know, to skulk there and not call out a civil greeting. Your papa bid me a 'Good day' this very noon, though like them all he would be glad to see me gone."

Jo and Nell stared at each other, amazed. How had she seen them when she had not even looked their way? And who did she think they were? They stood slowly, and were moving out from behind their brushy screen when Ellen Hawke caught sight of them. Her face froze, then lit up in fierce delight with as dazzling a smile as Nell's Granty's, but at the same time her hand shot out in warning— *Keep back!*— and the girls obeyed. Then, on the slope below the track, a tall man stepped from the shadows under a giant pine tree.

He was young. Dressed in a butternut-colored coat and breeches, and bareheaded, he wore his hair pulled back and tied in a queue. He carried a flintlock rifle across his arm.

"Good day, then, Mistress Hawke," he said, "and good morrow."

"Stay. You'll find no deer on this hillside today," Ellen Hawke said. "But there are two-footed rabbits and wolves. Stand quiet where you are, and see." She gave a whistle, and the dogs and horses left the road, ambling down into the shadows to stand as still as stones. When Jo looked away and then back again, for a moment she could not see where they stood. The man stepped back and vanished.

Soon, a faint sound of panting, of deep, ragged breathing, could be heard coming from downhill. As the panting grew louder, it was mingled with sobs and, just as the girls made out a flicker of movement, snatches of a woman's voice.

"*M'sieu Dieu, je vous prie . . . le Diable, il avait le cheval . . . j'ai seulement mes pauvres pieds . . . ah, M'sieu le bon Dieu, donnez-moi les ailes . . .*"

"What's she saying?" Jo hissed.

"Something about praying for wings," Nell whispered. "She—" Nell broke off as a black-skinned woman in a faded brown dress and gray shawl and cap, carrying a small bundle, came stumbling barefoot into view. She stopped to catch her breath, but as she did, a distant drum of hoofbeats floated up the air. She whirled. "*Ah! Je suis perdu!*" she sobbed, and ran on.

Moments later, the hoofbeats sounded close at hand, and a tall, bay horse plunged into view. Its rider was a large man with powder-white hair tied back in a queue, face flushed, and lips a line as thin as a razor blade. Hatted and booted, he wore a black coat and breeches, and carried a short whip he used to lash the horse's rump.

"Wretch!" he called. "Run off from master and mistress, will you, you nugacious gizzard of a nothing? Insignificant wart of a female! You'll not try it again, I warrant," he cried. Overtaking her, he raised his whip and brought it down across her shoulders again and again.

"Oh, stop!" Nell shrieked. "Stop it. Stop it!" Jo lunged after her as she scrambled out from their shelter.

The rider whirled his horse to face them, and gaped. "Save us!" he croaked. "Two imps of Satan the copy of that devil's handmaid, the woman Hawke." He turned back to glare at the woman who cowered before him.

"I knew it! Confess it! It was the woman Hawke who tempted you away."

"No, master. I not run away," the woman whimpered. "I bring herbs to sell to wise woman, goldenthread and snakeroot, and—"

"Hold your tongue! 'Tis a lie. 'Tis clothing in that bundle, and no herbs. Your 'wise woman' has lured you away, and I shall have the law on her for it. If these she-whelps of hers interfere, they may taste my whip, too." He sneered as he snatched at the bundle.

The Wise Woman

The ragged shawl came untied as the man pulled at it, spilling out handfuls of roots and a sheaf of green cuttings. If the master was surprised, the woman was astonished, but she hid her confusion quickly, and fear took its place.

Furious, the man dismounted and pulled a coil of rope from his saddlebag. He knotted a loop in one end, passing it over the woman's head, and tied the other end to his saddle horn. Swift as a snake, he was mounted again and off at a trot back down the road, with the slave woman lurching behind. He did not look back, and so he did not see the young man slip out from the trees to stare after him with a grim smile.

"Now we have you, Parson! We could not be rid of you for your pride and greed, but wicked cruelty is a stronger matter." He looked around for Ellen Hawke, but neither she nor her horses were anywhere to be seen. He shivered, and with an uneasy laugh set off downhill in pursuit of the parson.

"'Parson'? That was the *preacher?*" Nell whispered.

Jo did not answer. She was staring at the bundle abandoned in the road. The roots and herbs she had seen spill from the shawl were gone— vanished— and a pair of worn shoes, a ragged shift, and a patched skirt lay in their place.

"Quick!" She pushed Nell ahead of her. "We have to get back home. *Quick!*"

A Lost Room

In the downstairs back hallway of Winterbloom House— Nell's Winterbloom— Nell held the candlestick while Jo buckled a borrowed belt snugly around her waist and pulled the skirt of the plaid dress up through it to shorten it to knee length. Then she turned and eased the backdoor bolt free.

"I wish we could have stayed," Nell whispered in a rush. "Ellen Hawke saw us. Granty must have looked a lot like her when she was young. Couldn't we at least have talked to her? Oh, I wish you wouldn't go. I wish you would stay 'til morning. There's such a lot I don't understand. Why does it matter when you go back, if time's not like time in *Rip Van Winkle,* and you won't go back to find years and years are gone?"

"Because." Jo slipped out past her to the terrace.

A Lost Room

"Because moon-window time *is* real time, sixty seconds to a minute." She pulled up her lace cuff to peer at her watch. "And it's after midnight."

She stood for a moment, staring at Nell's face, then turned and ran along the terrace toward the elm tree. "Thanks for the belt," she called back softly.

"Good night— Cousin," Nell whispered.

Halfway up the elm, Jo thought she saw a glint of light close below. Startled, she shrank in against the trunk, and looked down to the right, toward the second-floor window directly below her own. A faint light glimmered on the panes, as if a lighted candle burned close by. She did not move for several moments, and took care to be quiet when she began to climb again.

Safely back in the attic, she stood for a moment in the dark and thought about the candle in the window. The room must be Nell's Granty's, or the lawyer from Boston's if he had stayed the night. The puzzle was, what room was it? The Rose Bedroom was the last one down the hall on that side, but it was far too small to reach all the way to the corner. Granty's room at the front corner of the house had no window on that side. To have one, her room would have to be as wide as the whole east side of the house.

At the foot of the circular stairway, Jo stood in the third-floor hallway, and stared down to the bathroom door at the far end. In Nell's Winterbloom, when she had tiptoed with Nell up to the Yellow Bedroom, *she had seen no bathroom door next door.* Instead, there had been more hall at the end of the hall: more hall, and a window at its end. In the candlelit darkness, she had not seen whether there was a window at the end of that second-floor hallway. The present-day second floor had its bathroom on the left, between the Green and Rose bedrooms. The far end of its hall, just beyond the Rose Bedroom door, was just the far end of the hall, with no window. So, the second-floor window below her own should belong to the Rose Bedroom. Somehow that didn't seem quite right, but Jo was too tired to think why it mattered. It could wait until the morning.

She was in bed and slipping into sleep when she stirred, remembering that in the morning she ought to be out the front door and away as soon as it was light . . . no, that was wrong. She had decided to go back to a year ago, and write herself a letter . . . or had there been something—

She slept.

Jo awoke at seven from an uneasy dream, and for a long while sat sleepy-eyed on the edge of the high bed and tried to remember what it was that she had told herself in her dream to remember. Whatever it was, it was lost, so finally she gave up and climbed down to pad across to the wardrobe, and then to the bathroom. She dressed and washed, and was brushing her teeth when she remembered the candle she had seen in the second-floor window the night before, in Nell's time. She frowned at herself in the mirror. The window hadn't been in her dream, and she didn't see how it could be important, but it bothered her. At least, since the hour was early, it was a puzzle she could solve before breakfast.

She began at the bathroom door. Stepping carefully, heel to toe, she measured off the hallway: fifty-four "Jo feet." She figured quickly in her head. That made something like thirty-six real feet. Counting the bathroom, the inside of the house must be about forty-six feet long. She made her way silently down to the second floor, and peered around the corner of the stairwell. The door to Granty's sitting room was closed. Since the only door into Granty's bedroom was through the sitting room, and since the Winterbloom walls were thick, Jo felt safe in tiptoeing down to the end of the hall and measuring her way back. It came out to forty-nine and a half heel-to-toe feet: shorter than the upstairs hall by about a yard. That was odd, perhaps, but hardly mysterious. If Granty had her private bathroom tucked into the end-of-hall space, directly below the third-floor bathroom, that only meant hers was a bigger bathroom. It was the little Rose Bedroom that provided the mystery.

Moon Window

The Rose Bedroom's door was on the left, right at the end of the hall, and it opened inward, flat against the room's side wall. The room ended where the hall ended. The Rose Bedroom was not the corner room after all. So what was?

From the terrace, Jo looked up and counted the second-floor windows along the back face of the house. There should have been one apiece for the two bedrooms and one for the bathroom between them, but instead, there were four. Around the corner, on the east side of the house, the only full-sized window, near the front corner, belonged to Granty's bedroom. Next to it was a small one like that belonging to the bathroom on the third floor. Further to the right, a faint outline and a slightly different color to the stonework suggested that once there had been a full-sized window—no, *two* full-sized walled-up windows between the little window and the corner. Odd . . .

Returning to the terrace, Jo took a folded piece of paper and a pencil from her pocket and plumped herself down in a wicker patio chair. Her first try at a diagram of the second floor didn't make sense, so she crossed it out and tried again.

It still wouldn't come right. She pulled her feet up to sit cross-legged and frown at the window just

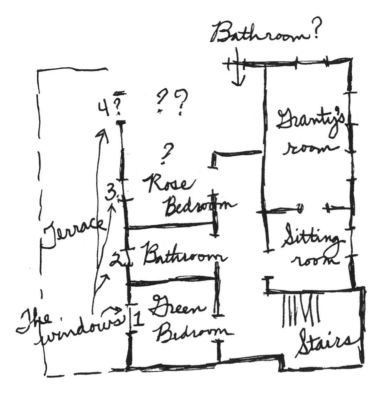

below her own: the extra window. It was open several inches at the top. From below it was impossible to see more than the top and sides of the deep window recess, and a shadowed scrap of ceiling, but if she were to climb into the elm tree . . .

It was when she tilted her head back to look straight up, that she discovered why she could see the window at all from where she sat. There was no leafy lowest branch to block her view. The lowest branch was off to the right and well out of reach, a good ten feet off the ground.

Jo almost fell off the chair in her haste to untangle her legs. Standing back from the tree and peering upward, she could see that, in several places where branches should have been— where she was sure they had grown— there were none. Heavy boughs *had* grown there, but they were gone. Peering up through the leaves, she could see the scars where, long ago, they had been sawn off close to the great trunk and then healed over. Alarmed, she backed further along the terrace, until she could see the turret.

No branch arched out to touch the moon window's stone sill.

In the turret room, the puzzle proved more puzzling still. Kneeling at the window, a breathless Jo could make out green leaves and the branch as before, through the wavy, sparkling glass. When she leaned into the deep recess to unlatch and open the window, it *was* there, bare, but as stout and strong as ever. Cold air bit at her hands on the window frame.

The elm's branches were gone, but not gone. How could that be? Jo shut her eyes and rubbed them with her cold palms, trying to sort it all out. The branch had been there the night before, when she climbed down to watch Nell's— Granty's— birthday party. That must mean that the branches had been cut away some time after 1897, so that now they existed only in the past. But when? And why?

Winterbloom House was growing stranger day by day.

Down below, a deer picked its way across a garden deep in snow.

At breakfast, Jo looked up from buttering her toast to dart a glance across the table, and shivered. *Granty was Nell!* Or used to be. It was a strange thought no matter which way you looked at it. The long-ago Nell had been so eager for adventure— too eager. What had happened to make her into an old lady afraid to go into town? It was going to be hard not to let on, not to ask.

"Are you all right, dear?"

Jo, startled, blinked. "What?"

"You shivered," Granty said. "You're not coming down with a summer cold, are you?"

"No." Jo shook her head and concentrated on spreading her marmalade evenly. "No, I was just thinking." With her head still down she added, as if she were only making conversation, "Granty? That little painting in my room— it's of a house exactly like this one, isn't it?"

It was Granty's turn to be startled. Her silver earrings trembled, and her long fingers fiddled with her rings. "Little painting? What little painting is that?"

Jo looked up. "You know. The little one of the misty valley with the sort of castle-ish house. You had Mrs. Craig hang it up in the Yellow Bedroom. It has something to do with Winterbloom, doesn't it?"

Granty picked up her coffee cup in both hands and took a large sip before she answered. "*That* painting. I'd forgotten. Yes, it's very old. I understand the first Ellen Macallan painted it herself, that it was meant to be her old home in the north of Scotland." She took another swallow of coffee. "I'm told the house was known as 'Castle MacAlpin.'"

"'MacAlpin'?" Jo was puzzled.

"Yes," Granty said, putting her cup down carefully. "Would you do another piece of toast for me, my dear?"

Jo went to the toaster, on the sideboard, to put in two slices of bread, and Granty said, "Yes. That was Ellen's real name, not Macallan. I'm afraid I know very little more about her Scottish home. After her father died, she became Lady Dewar and lived near Edinburgh, and when her husband died, she married a rich London merchant named Hawke. It was after he died, too, that she came to America. Like many people who came to start new lives here, she changed her name, but only by taking back her own name and changing the spelling a bit."

Jo thought for a moment, then chose her words carefully. "But whoever built this house must have known more than the picture shows. Winterbloom looks— *real*. Not like something invented from look-ing at tiny squiggles of paint."

Granty appeared confused. "I don't know. Perhaps. This house was built much later, most of it after the Revolutionary War. The stone was brought from Ver-mont, by raft and oxcart, I know, but . . . Wait— I do remember that the man who built it drew a set of plans. I believe I saw them in the attic many years ago. Perhaps he had seen other old drawings."

"Mm-m." This time Jo noticed Granty's nervous ring-twisting. As she popped up to bring the fresh toast, she fished wildly for a change of subject. "Do you have an encyclopedia?"

Granty blinked uncertainly. "Only an old one-volume one. What is it that you want to look up?"

"Well— the aura-whatsis. The Northern Lights."

"The aurora borealis? Whatever for?" Granty was even more bewildered.

"I— I think I saw it last night."

"Are you sure?" Granty asked. "It's usually in March or October that we see it here. But if you want the encyclopedia, I think you'll find it on the bottom shelf of the bookcase in the Great Hall."

Jo took the big, fat encyclopedia to the window seat overlooking the terrace and read while she kept an eye out for Granty. When the old lady ap-peared with her gardening basket and set out across the lawn for the flower border, Jo slipped down quickly and hurried out across the entry hall and upstairs.

She looked in the second-floor bathroom first. Guest hand towels hung on the towel rack, and a still-wrapped cake of soap sat in the soap dish. The medicine cabinet held only a clean glass. Clearly, Granty must have a bathroom of her own.

The sitting-room door and the door through into Granty's bedroom stood open. Jo stepped in quickly and looked around. She felt a twinge of guilt about snooping, but how else was she to find out about the corner room? Even if there really were old floor plans somewhere in the attic, it might take days to find them.

The window overlooking the drive in front, and the other, facing the side garden and the morning sun, were open wide. The canopy bed, its bedclothes neatly pulled down to air the sheets, stood with its head toward the inner wall. That entire wall was hung, from floor to ceiling and one end to another, with the panels of a tapestry landscape. On Jo's first peek into the room, the afternoon she came, it had been in shadow. Its colors, which must once have been bright as jewels, were dusty and faded, but the crowding trees and jagged hills, and birds and beasts, knights and ladies, were still magical to see. As Jo's fingers brushed the silken tail of a small red fox, she almost forgot what she had come for, but then caught herself, and frowned.

A Lost Room

She began her search with the furthest panel of the tapestry, between the corner of the room and the bed-post. There, an iron bracket curved out from the corner in the perfect place to hold a heavy pulled-back wall hanging, and so Jo tugged the tapestry aside and hung it there. The door behind it stood temptingly ajar. Beyond it was what she had expected: a bathroom much like the one directly above. It was a little larger, so that there was room for a small chest of drawers. Other than that, the only difference seemed to be the smell of lavender dusting powder, and the fat pottery cookie jar that sat atop the chest. Jo resisted the temptation to lift the lid and look inside. Backing out, she unhooked the tapestry to let it drop back into place.

On the other side of the bed, Jo peered behind another tapestry panel, and found a second door, but as she reached out to turn its handle, she heard the whiny hum of the stair elevator, carrying Granty's midmorning snack up for her. There was just enough time to reach the stairs and be on her way down as Granty reached the second landing.

While Granty took her morning nap, Mrs. Craig was on the third floor, dusting and vacuuming. Jo thought she could slip up and across the hall to the attic stair, but when she tried, she found the house-keeper using the vacuum-cleaner extension to clean the attic steps. Jo settled for exploring out-of-doors instead. In the hour or so before lunch, she first poked around the barn, eerily like and unlike the house-and-barn it once had been, and then along the stone wall near it, where she found a narrow gate. Past the gate, a narrow pathway led fifty or sixty yards to the Craigs' small house, which had its own driveway leading down the hill. Looking back toward Winterbloom, she was glad to see that the Craigs' windows had a clear view through the trees, across the wall, and through a gap in the orchard to Granty's bedroom window. She wondered whether they kept an eye out for a light there at night. The more she thought about it, the more odd it was that they didn't live in the house itself. With six empty bedrooms, it seemed silly.

When Jo returned to the house just before lunchtime, Granty was in the kitchen, watching as Mrs. Craig opened the oven to check on a pie.

"It smells lovely! Oh, Jo, there you are. I have a question for you. I should have thought of it yesterday. Would you like to telephone your mother in France? With the time difference, it will be just after six in the evening there now. They won't have gone out to dinner yet."

Jo stared. "Yes. Yes, I'd like that," she said numbly.

She had completely forgotten her mother and George.

Old Memories

"More oyster pie?" Granty asked.

Jo nodded absently. She was trying to understand how she could actually, after saying good-bye to her mother, have added "Say 'Hi' to George."

"I've been fretting ever since yesterday—" Granty said. Her hand was not quite steady as she dished out a large spoonful of steaming pie. "Fretting about your missing out on our expedition to old Fort No. 4. To make it up to you, I've asked Young Tom to take you down to the Thirkells' this afternoon. Theirs is the farm at the the bottom of the hill. Young Alice and Louisa have cousins visiting, and they're taking them up to the old fort. The Thirkell girls are quite nice children, Mrs. Craig says, and I'm sure their cousins are, too. How does that sound to you?"

Jo was glad she had her mouth full and could not answer for a moment, because she felt like saying *"Boring!"* She almost groaned, but when she saw how anxious Granty looked, she swallowed, and managed to mumble, "Fine, I guess."

At half past one, Granty waved young Mr. Craig and an unenthusiastic Jo on their way as the big old car rolled out the drive.

Granty went directly to the Great Hall, in search of her reading glasses, and saw the encyclopedia lying open on the window seat.

"Now, how *can* the child have seen the Northern Lights from her room?" she asked aloud as she crossed the room. "The elm trees block out the northern sky."

The book, she saw, was not open to *Aurora borealis,* but to the pages covering *Fremantle* to *French literature.* Curious, Granty ran her finger down the columns to see what or whom Jo might have been looking up. Surely not Mr. Fremont, Fremstad, or Fremy, or General John Denton Pinkstone French . . . Her finger hesitated over *French and Indian Wars* and, as it did, the uneasiness that had been growing since breakfast deepened into dread. She did not know why. The day outdoors was warm and all of the windows stood open, but she felt chilled to the bone. She read the long entry carefully, looking for some reason for her alarm, but found none. But why should a child, out of the blue, be curious about the American battles and Indian raids of a war between Britain and France that ended in 1763? Granty's finger had moved on to *French Broad River* when she suddenly snatched it away with a gasp.

1763 . . . 1764.

1764. The dream.

The dream, so long buried, came flooding back: the dream about stepping through the moon window. After it happened, she had told herself it was a dream, a daydream, because how could it have been real? The old barn. The Indian Joshark. The man beating the slave woman, and Ellen watching. And— Joanna. Only after she came back to Winter- bloom to stay had she come to know it was no dream.

Granty reached out unsteadily for the corner of the piano. Joanna. *Jo was Joanna.*

Jo was Joanna!

"Oh, no! Not Jo." She sank weakly onto the piano bench. "I should have remembered. I knew there was something. When I saw her in my plaid dress, oh, why didn't I remember?"

Mrs. Craig appeared in the doorway. "Did you call me, Miss Mac?"

"Did I—" Granty looked at the housekeeper blankly for a moment, but then nodded. "Yes, Jean. I'll go up early for my rest, I think."

"Right. I'll have your tray ready in two shakes.

There's a poppyseed cake, but it's still in the oven. Will sugar cookies do?"

"Sugar— oh, yes," Granty said. Her mind was not on food.

For the first time, Granty did not climb the stairs to the second floor, but rode, sitting pale and upright with the tray on her lap. Twenty minutes later, wearing bootee slippers and clutching a ring of keys so that they would not jingle, she padded out through her sitting room and around the corner to the stairs.

She climbed slowly, careful not to tire herself, and rested for a moment on the third-floor landing, then turned down the hallway toward the open door of the Yellow Bedroom. As she stood in the bedroom doorway, her eyes searched the walls, and when she saw the little portrait of Ellen in her green gown, she grew paler still.

"Oh, dear, that too!" she whispered. "And the little stool. But how?" When she spied the little painting of Castle MacAlpin, she closed her eyes, and turned back down the hallway.

The door at the foot of the stair to the attic was unlocked. It should not have been. The old lady gave the steep steps an anxious look, then sat down on the second step to rest and gather courage. She reached the top by one slow step at a time. At the door of the tower room above the main staircase, she tried to turn its key in the lock, but nothing happened. It was already unlocked. She had half expected that, but still was puzzled for hers was the only key. Inside, most of the furnishings that had long ago been moved here from the turret room were untouched, but a neat, dustless triangle marked where the little needlework stool, wrapped in newspaper, had stood atop a table. Where the two small paintings had hung, now there were only two light patches on the wall.

The door to the little turret room was unlocked, too, and its long-dusty floor was crisscrossed with footprints. A little heap of paint dust and chips beside the baseboard nearby caught her eye. Trembling, Granty stooped to peer at the window and saw the neat cut that freed it from its frame. She was too late. She had removed the paintings and furnishings from the turret room long ago, and locked the doors. She had painted the window shut and had the limbs cut from the tree. Nothing had helped. Jo had already stepped into the web.

Granty helplessly stood twisting the rings on her thin hands. What else could she have done? What should she do next?

She made her way back to the stairway and worked her way downward, stopping every few steps to rest. When at last she reached the second floor, she made her way even more cautiously through the sitting room to reach her bed.

Later. She would decide later what to do.

At 3:45, Granty opened her eyes, sat up, and reached for the telephone on the bedside table.

"Tom?" she said after a moment. "When did Mrs. Thirkell say you should go to pick up Jo? Five o'clock? Good, that will give me time for a cup of tea. Then I think I shall ride down and back with you. No, no—I shall be fine. It's quite near. I would like to thank Mrs. Thirkell myself, and perhaps I shall take her one of your mother's poppyseed cakes. Yes, that's just what I shall do. A quarter to five, then? Thank you, Tom."

When she had replaced the receiver, old Miss Macallan sat still for a long while, until her heart stopped racing. Then she rose, changed into her blue dress, reached the blue straw hat down from the wardrobe shelf, and went downstairs to her tea.

When the old black Packard pulled out from the Winterbloom lane onto the hill road, Granty leaned forward to tap Young Tom on the shoulder.

"Tom, pull over to the side, please. Yes, right here."

Tom Craig braked to a stop and turned quickly. "Something wrong, Miss Mac?"

"No, no, Tom. But there's a very important long-distance call to Colorado that I must make. Do you have your little pocket telephone with you? If I'm right about the time difference, Jo's grandparents will have left for the airport if I wait until we get back to the house."

"The cell phone? Sure, Miss Mac. What's the number? I'll get it for you." When Jo's grandmother came on the line, he handed the cellular phone back to Miss Macallan.

"Peggy? It's Granty. You're not on your way out the door already, are you? I was afraid I'd be too late . . . No, dear, I'm fine, and Jo's fine. It's just that something has come up, some business I have to attend to, that will make it difficult for me to have Jo here for as long as I would like . . . Good heavens, no! She's being a perfect guest, and entertaining herself. I nap such a lot that she has to do so . . . Thank you, dear. That's just what I hoped you'd say. Now, I know you're about to leave for California. When do you fly back to Denver? . . . What time on Sunday?"

Granty took a small notebook and pencil from her handbag as Mrs. Lucas repeated her question to Mr. Lucas. "Half past five. What airline and flight number? . . . Good. There must be a flight that will get Jo in close to then. Young Tom can drive her to Manchester Airport, and she can get a connecting flight in Boston or Pittsburgh. When young LuAnn came last summer, the airline's people looked after her between flights."

She listened for a moment. "No, my dear, don't call me. Give me the name of your hotel, and I'll call you . . . Yes. And have a lovely trip. Give my best to Henry. Good-bye, my dear."

Granty peered at the buttons on the little telephone. "Tom? How do I 'hang up'?"

Young Tom reached back. "Here, give it t'me, Miss Mac."

Granty handed over the phone, then jotted down the hotel's name, and leaned back in her seat. "Now, don't you forget to let me know how much the call cost, Tom. And, Tom? I think I won't tell Jo just yet. No need to spoil the rest of her time here."

Tom Craig turned the ignition key. "Sure, Miss Mac."

Sunday, she was thinking. *Wednesday, Thursday, Friday, and Saturday to go.*

A Whisper in the Dark

At dinner, Granty put on a cheerful face, and laughed as she told about Old Tom's latest garden invention, a spring-loaded kneeling stool that, when he had finished weeding the onion rows, had not boosted him to his feet as it was meant to, but tipped him over into the radishes. Even as she tried to sparkle, there was an air of sadness Jo could not miss. It was something new to her, to feel the feelings that lay hidden under words. It was— uncomfortable.

"Granty, if you're unhappy here, why stay?" she blurted out before she could stop herself.

Granty, startled, shrugged and answered just as simply, "Because I cannot go."

Jo frowned. "Because of your aggrophobia? That's what Mrs. Craig said it was."

This time Granty's laugh was genuine. "'Aggrophobia'! I like the sound of that: a 'fear of being aggravated.' But I think what she meant was 'agoraphobia.' That means a 'dread of open spaces.'"

She looked down and took a tiny bite of ice cream. "It's not quite true, though. I enjoy being out in the garden, and sometimes still visit other parts of the property. It's the house, you see. When I was younger, I could go into Walpole without fretting about— about being away from it. Now I cannot."

Jo did not see at all or, rather, she saw that Granty, if she had a reason, did not mean to share it.

"It must be hard in winter," Jo said, giving up and changing the subject. "With no central heating, I mean."

"Oh, yes!" The old lady was clearly relieved to talk of other things. "We close off the third floor and have to keep fires going all day in the downstairs fireplace stoves, or the cold creeps as deep into the bones of the house as it does into mine. When I had bathrooms put in, the pipes had to go up the outside of the house because the walls are solid stone, and even when they are insulated, pipes freeze. After winter truly sets in, we drain them and turn to the old hand pump at the kitchen sink. That means, alas, that we must go back to the old ways: heating bathwater on the stove and using chamber pots." She smiled.

Jo frowned. "But don't you hate it?"

A Whisper in the Dark

Granty was amused. "Of course. Once upon a time, when I was small, modern bathrooms were still a town luxury, and it may have taken almost a hundred years for some farmhouses to catch up, but I have never hankered after the 'good old days.' Still, if a bit of inconvenience was enough to drive me away, I would have left Winterbloom long before Peggy— your grandmother— was born." Her smile was wistful, as if she wished she had.

After dinner, Jo and Granty played a game of checkers, which Jo suspected Granty could have won much sooner than she did. Then Granty settled down to her jigsaw puzzle, and Jo returned to the book she had begun on her first evening at Winterbloom. This time as she turned the pages, she was thinking of jigsaw puzzles, for it seemed to her that Winterbloom's mystery was just that. There must be a secret that explained the moon window and the lost room and Granty's being almost a prisoner, but Jo had too few pieces of the puzzle to solve it. Where to look for more, except through the moon window, was a puzzle itself. The moon window frightened her. Some tiny thing she had done or said on the other side of the window might already have changed the present. She would never know.

Granty collected her tray with its thermos jug and slice of cake, and went up to bed soon after the Great

Hall grew shadowy enough for the lamps to be turned on. Jo stayed behind, still puzzling, until the dusk outside was almost darkness. Then she unfastened the back door and slipped out. From the shadows under the elm tree, she looked up at the window overlooking the terrace from the "lost room" and saw the flicker of light she was looking for.

"If there's always a light," she whispered to herself, "and if the side windows around the corner weren't blocked up, the Craigs would see it from their house." Perhaps that was why the side windows had been walled up: so that whoever lived in the little house could not see lights in an "empty" room. The stonework was not fresh. It could be fifty or a hundred years old, or older. If she asked the question the right way— "When?" and not "Why?"— Granty might answer it. One more puzzle piece to try to fit into place.

And she would *not* go up to the attic.

At least, not at night . . .

At nine-thirty, *Five Children and It* slid from Jo's bed to the floor, and she awoke with a start. "But it *wasn't* their fault," she mumbled drowsily as she groped for the little dangling on-off chain on the bed-side lamp. Yet as she pulled it and nestled her head deeper into her pillow, sleep drew away like a wave slipping back down a beach into the sea, and she seemed to hear at her ear the troublesome whisper that had drawn her into the past to cross James Russell's path. *Why are you abed? The puzzle is waiting for you. All the past yours to explore. Why fear it?*

Jo stirred drowsily. Her mind was awake, but it was as if her body still slept. She could not make it sit up, or open its eyes, but her ears seemed to hear movement in the air, and her skin felt it stir above her face. After a long moment, she managed to force her eyes open and see that there was no one but her-self in the moonlit room. Once she was able to move her head and then sit up on the edge of the bed, she saw that the door into the hall stood open. She was sure— half sure?— that she had closed it.

At the other end of the hall, the door at the foot of the circular stair stood open too. Barefoot, she ran to stand on the bottom step and listen for sounds above. Nothing stirred. "I could go up and only look," she told herself. "It can't hurt just to look." She padded back to the bedroom for her slippers and the little flashlight.

The door to the turret room was open wide, and the moon window's bolt moved easily for once. Jo pushed the window open gingerly and looked out upon the rock-walled northern valley in the hour before dawn. The full moon floated low over the scrap of sea at the valley's end, and shadows filled the channel of the stream and the hollows in the hills. Below, where before she had seen only rocks and bare earth, a small garden grew with pines and hedges, and moon-green grass, but here and there the shadows of the pines and hedge shrubs stirred. As her eyes became accustomed to the gloom, she saw figures hiding there, and in the hollows further off, and along the stream. On its far bank and up out of sight on her right, light from some unseen source flickered and died among the rocks.

Jo leaned out to look straight down. The windows below were dark, but from somewhere indoors she seemed to hear an odd, low rumble. Then a sharp whistle shrilled, and the light grew golden-red and brighter. Three floors below, the back door opened and a woman carrying a lamp rushed out, and after her a second, like her, dark-gowned and aproned. Between them they pulled a third, who struggled and protested, and cried out.

"Father! Father!" the third called in panic, and turned her face up to the moon window as she twisted away.

Her face was Ellen's, the young Ellen of the green gown and the smile. As the women forced her across the garden and down the slope beyond, she screamed out again, "Father!" Then the wind shifted, and Jo smelled smoke. Beyond the garden dark figures rose up to flee, and off to the right torches bobbed into view and away as the torchbearers fled along the stony stream. And with the change of wind the muffled rumble became a roar, and Jo saw that the flickering red glow had become a golden glare that lit all the valley. From below came the sound of cracking windowpanes, and then smoke roiled upward from the lower floors.

Castle MacAlpin was ablaze.

Ellen

Jo slammed the window shut, and then the door to the tower room as she stumbled down the three steps into the main attic. There, she sat on a wooden box and coughed and wiped her stinging eyes until she could see to follow the beam of her pocket light to the stairway. The light was growing dim, and so she switched it off, and felt her way down the circular stair.

What did it all mean?

Jo sat on the bottom step. Winterbloom House was silent except for the drumming of her heart. What did it all mean? She had seen Castle MacAlpin burned down by enemies, yes. But the young Ellen had escaped— been forced to escape. *The young Ellen* . . . On the far side of the moon window Jo had

138

Ellen

now seen a young Ellen, one somewhere between youth and middle age, and one, Nell's Granty, who was old. Each had the same wild, hawk-eyed beauty, and on two she had seen the same vivid smile. The same spellbinding smile . . .

They were all the same woman.

"That's crazy!" Jo whispered to herself. As she thought about the past two days, the idea seemed both stranger still, and more likely to be true. Ellen *was* a spellbinder. She had turned the slave woman's poor rags into herbs. She had built a house with a strange bronze wheel of a window marked with unreadable writing— what else but a spell? And Granty was surely spellbound, or she would have sold Winterbloom House and left long ago. Jo felt eerily as if she were a piece in some unseen board game, being pushed from riddle to answer to riddle. But who was the player and what was the game?

And how do I push back?

Jo stood in her stocking feet in the second-floor hallway, and peered in through the open door of Granty's sitting room. The curtains were open, and the moonlight in the room showed that the bedroom door was wide open, too. To Jo's eyes, accustomed to the dark, the moonlight and the tiny night lamp glowing on old Miss Macallan's bedside table made the room seem almost bright. Granty's bedspread and summer blanket were folded neatly over the foot of the bed, and she lay stretched out flat, the sheet pulled up to her chest. A china saucer on the table held her rings, and her thin but beautiful long-fingered hands lay at her sides. Her breathing was loud and even, as if she were in the deepest pool of sleep. Jo padded over to the tapestry on the wall and felt her way along it to the opening between the panels. If the door to the lost room were locked, at least she would have tried.

But it was not. It was not even closed, and a faint breeze that stirred the heavy silk and woollen hanging carried with it the scent of rosemary and oranges. Jo held her breath and slipped behind the tapestry to stand astonished in the doorway.

Candles— strangely, electric candles— glimmered dimly on a heavy silver candelabra-lamp on a table between the two windows. The room was furnished with a deep, high-backed armchair, a broad, low stool, a shoulder-high carved cupboard, and a wide poster bed with curtains tied back with tasseled cords. The room appeared empty. Jo took a hesitant step forward, and felt carpet underfoot.

"Close the door, my dear. Your Granty will not wake, but close the door."

The silvery voice was so delicate and distant that Jo thought at first she had imagined it. She looked nervously toward the back of the armchair, which faced the candlelight, and then to the shadowy bed, but still saw no one.

"Yes, JoEllen, here."

The paper-thin voice did come from the bed. Uncertainly, Jo reached back to close the door, and then stepped closer. In the shadows under the bed canopy, propped up by cushions and pillows, lay a figure so slight that she seemed hardly to be there. White hair, still thick, lay in a long braid over her shoulder. Like the thin hands, only white skin and slender bone, that lay atop the bedcovers, her face seemed little more than a transparent image in the shadows. But the dark eyes were large and bright and eager.

"Ah, good welcome to you, lass! I have been waiting so many long years. I knew that you would come, but not when."

Jo took a nervous step back. "What do you mean?" she whispered. "Who are you?"

"Don't be afraid. I am Ellen Macallan. I'm your Granty's cousin— *her* own 'Granty,' as she still calls me. Does that seem strange to you?"

Jo's throat tightened, and she could not speak. She shook her head.

"No? Not strange? But you do not believe it. Why?"

Jo swallowed, and words came out in a whispery croak. "Because you're the first Ellen. You're Ellen

MacAlpin— the first and all the Ellens since, except for Granty."

The room was silent for a long moment, and then the thin shadow-hand stretched out. "Come closer, Ellen."

"JoEllen," Jo protested, but the dark eyes drew her slowly to the side of the bed. Half fearfully, she took the hand that reached out to her, and found it not cold and wrinkled, but cool and smooth, like silky paper.

"Shall I tell you why I have had to wait for you?" The silvery voice had a lilting rise and fall to it, as if it were weaving a web with words. "It is because I have needed someone young to do what must be done before I can rest. Once, long ago, I stole something of value out of the past, and now that I am old, it preys upon my mind. To right the wrong, it must go back."

"But why wait so long? And why me?" Jo asked warily.

The dark eyes held her. "Because you and your Granty are the only children of The MacAlpin to discover that the past lies beyond the moon window. I could never pass through it because all I have ever seen through its circle are terrible flames. Your Granty was always too fearful of the window's height to do what I ask, but you— you have the courage, and know the danger of meddling in time. I can trust you to return it to its place and close the window on my old mistake." The old woman smiled. "One day Winterbloom will be yours, you know."

That smile was as warm and beautiful as Jo remembered. Jo was still wary, but dazzled even so.

"Mine? *Winterbloom?*"

"It must be someone's," the Ellen-shadow said. She brushed aside Jo's astonishment with a flutter of her hand. "I built it to remember by, but all it does is haunt me. Except for the moon window, which I brought from my old world, it is no better than a pasteboard castle fitted out with whittled chairs and beds, with acorn cups, and walnut shells for bowls. You like it because you have never seen the true house. My father built that in a wilderness of rock and water, on the rim of my mother's father's lands— but you have seen the place, I think."

Jo would have asked, "Your father— who was he?" but the shadow-Ellen answered the thought before she spoke the words. "My grandfather's people called him The MacAlpin. They came to him for doctoring, for weather warnings and readings from the stars, and other wisdoms. But they, like my grandfather the Earl, feared him for his knowledge and hated him for winning my mother away." The silver voice had a sharp edge of anger. "They called him Wizard, and in the end they burnt him. Three times in the years since, I escaped my own burning because I knew the danger signs in men's eyes, and moved on. I had and lost husbands, three of them, and had children, too, but they feared me for my strangeness, and took themselves away."

She shrugged and gave a little laugh. "So, now I bring my children's children's children back to learn whether The MacAlpin's blood still runs in living veins. Only two. In all these years, you and Nell have been the only two. In her it is weak, but in you . . ."

Jo felt as if a sinkhole were opening up at her feet, but she was too fascinated to step back.

"Go to the cupboard, child. Yes, there." The frail hand dropped Jo's to gesture toward the dark, carved cupboard that stood against the wall beyond the bed. "The compartment just under the top shelf— its key is in the little bowl beside it."

Jo made her way around the foot of the bed to peer at the cupboard's second shelf, where she found the bowl and the key.

"Open it, and bring me what you find."

Inside the carved door, Jo found what felt like a squarish object with rounded corners, wrapped in a rough fabric. When she lifted it to carry it across to the bed, it was surprisingly heavy.

"Here you are. But what is it? It's so heavy." Jo placed it beside Ellen MacAlpin's hand, where it sank deep in the featherbed.

The old woman's hand winced away from it. "No, place it on the shelf, lass. It weighs on me here," she said faintly. "As to what it is, inside the wrappings is a stone box, but what is in the box I must not tell you. It must go back where it belongs. It must be as if it had never been here." She watched narrowly as Jo turned it over curiously and then set it carefully upon the shelf. Then, with no change of voice, but with her hands plucking at the linen coverlet, she asked, "Tonight, when you watched at the moon window, you saw the fire, the fire that— burned the castle? I felt your fear."

"I saw you there," Jo whispered.

The thin hands clenched upon the coverlet. "Then you have seen why I have never been able to cross into the past and walk about in strange or happy times. When *I* look through the window, my mind is always full of flames, and my father trapped in his turret. I have courage, but not enough to join him in those flames."

"But you built this house, and put the window in it," Jo said.

"Ah." Two frail hands captured one of Jo's as the silken voice spun on. "If I could not have the past, I could re-create a bit of it at the edge of another wilderness, and wait for a son or daughter of our house who would do the thing I could not do." Old Ellen's eyes held Jo's, like one cat's will hold another's. "The box belongs to the time before the fire, and must return there. Not tonight, perhaps, but time grows short. Tomorrow. Yes, tomorrow, when you watch at the moon window, and call up the valley—"

"But I don't. I can't," Jo said helplessly. "The times just come."

Old Ellen went on as if she had not heard. "You must look to the outer wall just to the window's left, where you will see a basket hanging from a ring. At mealtimes, if my father is at his studies in the turret room and does not wish to be disturbed, he unties the rope and lets the basket down so we may send his food up. What you must do is to make sure the rope is securely tied, then place the box within the basket. It belongs inside the turret room in my father's time, but I can see no way to bring it there, except to let him find it in the basket." The dark eyes sought Jo's and held them fast as the voice faded. "You will do it? Say you will."

"If I can," Jo whispered. "Yes."

"But do not tell your Granty," the shadow-Ellen warned as Jo backed toward the door. "She is good-hearted, but too timid. She would fear for you even though this is a simple matter. But what could happen?"

As the door eased shut, Old Ellen drew a long breath, then closed her eyes and smiled.

"What indeed?"

The Stone Box

The stone box, in its tightly stitched woollen cover, sat on Jo's bedside table and troubled her sleep. In her dream she tossed and turned, tangling herself in the bedsheet, while on the table thin cracks of light glowed through the box's cover, jagged cracks that grew wider, stretching the cloth until both the stitching and the cloth began to tear . . .

Jo woke and sat up with a start and found that she really was tangled in the sheet. On the bedside table, the woollen parcel sat looking like nothing more than a parcel wrapped and stitched up in wool. Beside it, her alarm clock read only 11:40.

She knew one thing that was bothering her. Why had Old Ellen said, "Don't tell your Granty"? She hadn't told Granty anything at all yet, but now so much had happened, each thing stranger than the last, that she longed to. Had she actually promised not to? She could not remember.

She scowled at the stone box. "At least I can stop *you* glowering at me," she grumbled. Climbing down from the bed, she took the heavy little bundle across to the wardrobe and, spying the old knapsack, dumped out its contents and stuffed in the woollen parcel. Then she closed the wardrobe doors on it, and turned the key in the lock.

"There! *Now* can I get back to sleep?"

It was a long time coming.

Early the next morning, Jo woke from a dream in which Granty was chained to her own bedpost by a leash only long enough to allow her to sit by the window and watch the deer devour her beloved roses. The leash and collar were somehow all one piece, and though there was a keyhole in the collar, the key was nowhere to be found. Jo was looking in the cookie jar when she awoke.

The sun had not yet cleared the circling forest pine trees, but as she leaned out the east window of her room, Jo could see it gleaming in the top branches of the elm beside the terrace. She drew a deep breath. Might as well stop worrying and get it over with! She dressed, then brought the knapsack and stone box from the wardrobe. As she climbed to the attic, she hoped it would not take all day to reach Castle MacAlpin before the fire. Granty would be sure to wonder what was going on. Besides, she might have some new expedition planned. Perhaps— perhaps if you opened and closed the moon window quickly, time after time, past time would flicker back and forth from year to year. When— or if— it touched on Castle MacAlpin, you simply left the window open.

Castle MacAlpin. *Castle MacAlpin* . . . Jo thought fiercely as she crossed the attic to the turret door.

Castle MacAlpin, she thought as she took the stone box from the knapsack and set it on the deep windowsill. "Castle MacAlpin," she said aloud as she reached for the bolt knob and peered out through the wavy glass into grayness.

And the window opened onto the harsh northland valley in a drizzling rain.

Jo, in her surprise, half rose and bumped her head against the slanting curve of the deep window recess. Was that all it took? *Thinking* a time? Her taking after the MacAlpins, as Old Ellen had said, must be part of what made it work. But then— then, if you knew what the risks were, and were careful, *and* learned enough about the past to keep out of trouble, you could explore it. You could travel in it . . . *live* in it. *If* you knew enough about it: that was the hitch. But she could learn.

"One day Winterbloom will be yours, you know."

One day . . . The thought made Jo a little dizzy.

Moon Window

With an effort, Jo brought her mind back to the stone box. She craned out for a quick look along the wall to the left of the window, and saw why she would not have noticed the hanging basket in the darkness, or by firelight. Its rope was looped through an iron ring and tied just above eye level, at a long reach— a man's reach— from the window opening. The basket itself hung several feet below. Jo pulled her head back in to brush the rain from her face and shake her damp curls, but found to her surprise that they were quite dry.

She needed something with which to hook the rope so that she could pull the basket up. Out in the attic she poked through several boxes of odds and ends and came up with an old potato masher. When she came back to the moon window, the rain was more mist than drizzle, and so she set to work. The masher caught on the first try, and Jo hauled up the basket. She began to pull basket, rope, and all after her as she backed out to fetch the wrapped stone box, but then realized with a shock that her hand was empty. The willow basket, perfectly strong and whole a moment before, teetered on the window frame with a large gap in its near side. The rope she held had vanished too, though she could see a part of it beyond the window rim. Jo crouched for a baffled moment on the sill before the answer dawned on her.

Objects from the past could not cross into the

future. Not leaf dust or mud or rain or baskets . . .

Jo slipped down from the deep, slanted sill and stood. "Or Nell's belt!" she exclaimed. She had borrowed Nell's belt to shorten the plaid dress as she climbed the tree. She had not been wearing it when she undressed for bed, and she had not seen it in the attic or on the stair. Like the bit of basket and the rope it had simply stayed where it was, dropping to the terrace or catching on the long-ago window sill. But that would mean—

The spell woven by Old Ellen's silvery voice wavered.

"She *couldn't* have stolen the stone box *out* of the past," Jo whispered aloud. "Not the way she let me think." Not even if it were a lie about being afraid to use the window. The box had been with Ellen all along. Jo stared down at it mistrustfully in its homely wrapping.

What could be in it to make it so important?

And why send it into the past?

For a moment Jo did not move. When she did, it was to bend down and bundle the heavy parcel back into the knapsack. Climbing back onto the sill, she reached out to grasp the basket and rope, and push them free of the window.

Why send it into the past?

The Last Puzzle Piece

Granty, late down to breakfast, still had a puffy-eyed, sleepy look, and covered a yawn as she waited for her coffee to cool. Jo suspected that the old lady's long, deep slumber was Ellen Macallan's doing. She tried to imagine that frail shadow slipping sleeping pills into a bedside glass of milk while Granty Nell was in the bathroom, and couldn't. Perhaps she did it without stirring a finger, just by thinking it. The more Jo thought about the whispers in her mind that had nudged her deeper into Winterbloom's mystery, the more she mistrusted Old Ellen. "Witch Ellen." That nickname may have come down through the family because the old portrait in the Great Hall made her look as alarming as she was beautiful. It could just as easily have been because her Russell children knew the truth. What had Old Ellen said— that her children "took themselves away"?

After her cereal and toast and a second cup of coffee, Granty began to look brighter. "You seem very glum, Jo dear," she said. "Aren't you feeling well?"

Jo straightened in her chair and did her best to put on a cheerful face. "I'm fine, Granty. Just daydreaming."

"What is it to be this morning? Would you like to ride your bicycle down to the Thirkells'? Or you could invite them to go horseback riding. There is a riding stable south of town, by the river. Young Tom could drive you all down, and fetch you back up the hill afterward."

"No, I don't think so."

"Just as you like. I think I shall spend an hour or so pinching leaves on the apple trees. Thomas tells me we have a problem with leaf rollers, and if we wait too long, the larvae will become moths and lay still more eggs." There was a nervous hint of invitation in the way she said it.

Jo began moving the breakfast dishes to the tray on the sideboard. "I'll take these out to the kitchen and then come help," she declared.

"We can leave the upper branches to the two Thomases," Granty said as they moved into the orchard east of the house. "Now, you may either pinch the rolled-up leaf off and drop it in the bucket, or leave it on the tree and pinch along it to squash the larvae inside," she explained with a shadow of a smile.

"Eeyuh!" Jo exclaimed with a shudder. "I'll use the bucket."

They worked together in silence until they reached the tree nearest the path that led through the narrow gate in the stone wall to the Craigs' house. Then Jo touched Granty's wrist and nodded toward the gate.

"Nell?" she said.

Granty's eyes widened. Then she nodded, took her walking stick from against the tree trunk, and followed. Once the gate was closed behind them, she propped the stick against the wall and folded Jo in a girlish hug. "Oh, Joanna! I did remember. It took awhile, but I remembered." Then, suddenly anxious, she held Jo at arm's length to look at her. "What is it? Oh dear, you've seen her, haven't you? Ellen. Last night while I slept so soundly."

Jo threw an uneasy look at the gate and the rooftop visible over the orchard treetops. "Can we talk, or does she hear everything we say?"

Granty shook her head "No," but gave a shrug as she did so. "I've never been sure. But she has always seemed able to read my feelings."

Jo pulled from her pocket a slip of paper and gave it to Granty. She had written on it, *She asked me to do something.*

Granty wadded it up and stuffed it in her own pocket. "Shall we walk a little further?"

As they went, Jo's questions overflowed. "How can she *be* so old? Didn't people catch on? Who is she really?"

"She told me a little," Granty said slowly, choosing her words with care. As they came to a garden bench beside the path, she sat down with a thankful sigh. "And the moon window told me more. I was never able to climb down the tree, but I could watch and listen. I saw some strange folk. Part of her, I believe, is something older than human. Once many years ago, I looked up the name 'MacAlpin' in a book of surnames. 'Mac' means 'son of,' and the name is thought to mean 'the son of Elphin.'"

"*Elfin?*" Jo stared. "As in 'elves'?"

Granty nodded. "There are other Scottish tales of the First Folk and their half-children, and of old families descended from them. The MacAlpin, Ellen's father, seems to have been an amazing fellow, a scientist as much as a wizard. After his death, and the fire, Ellen went back with her grandfather's servants to dig through the ruins, and she came away with the copper window in its frame and, I gather, gold from the vaults below the house. Years later, from time to time the old tales— or new ones— of witchery caught up with her. In those times the law still burned witches, but she was wise. When she saw the uneasy, sideways looks begin, she sold her property and moved on. It was the same in New England until she came here."

Jo was still puzzled. "But people here had to see she wasn't getting older fast enough. What about the servants?"

Granty shrugged. "After our Mr. Russell was dead and her children gone, she became the hermit no one from outside ever saw. The Winterbloom servants have always been from somewhere else, not from hereabouts." Granty gave a short laugh. "At least once she shut up the house and sailed for Europe, returning years later as her own 'niece,' who had supposedly taken the name of Ellen Macallan to please her. The 'new' Ellen brought new servants. It was only when she began to feel old age creeping into her bones at last that she knew she could not play such tricks forever, that she would need a 'new Ellen' to deal with the servants and the outside world. For that, she stopped playing the hermit and set her Boston lawyers to tracing the descendants of the Russell children. That is how you and I came to be here. She had seen us, remember? She was looking for us."

"But—" Jo began.

Granty gave her head a warning shake and, drawing Jo's crumpled-up question from her pocket, held it up between her thumb and forefinger. "Dear me," she said, "it's almost time for my morning rest, and we haven't finished even two trees' worth of leaf rollers. Shall we go in? Do you know, I think I will ask Mrs. Craig to do us a picnic lunch. I can show you the spot where Ellen's first cabin stood, and where she first planned to build the house that would keep Castle MacAlpin alive for her. Young Tom will drive us." She reached out a hand for Jo to help her stand. "It's a perfect picnic day."

Half a mile north of Winterbloom House, not far past the point where the old Packard turned off Chapnook Hill Road into a narrow dirt lane, the car began to run unevenly, and soon was lurching and sputtering. "Sorry, Miss Mac," Tom Craig said as he switched off the ignition. "I don't know what's got into her. I tuned her up just last week. Soon as we get your picnic gear set out, I'll come back and take a look under the hood, and have my bite to eat later. It's not too far for you to walk, is it, Miss Mac?"

"No, not a bit, Tom," Granty assured him.

Ahead, the forest opened out into a long, wide clearing, invaded along its edges by a few younger trees. Granty made her way slowly, with the help of her walking stick, to an old stone foundation, a rectangle enclosing a space where the grass had been kept roughly cut. Jo followed, carrying her old knapsack like a shoulder bag, clutched tightly to her side.

"I come here often," Granty explained as Young Tom set up a folding picnic table and armchairs and helped Jo unpack the lunch. "This was the foundation of the log house Ellen first lived in. She meant one day to build Winterbloom in the middle of the clear-ing, but then she had a well dug and when the diggers reached water, it was brown and peaty. Even though the clearing felt firm underfoot, it had been an ancient bog— still is, a bit, down toward the south end. A great stone house, even one with deep foundations, would have shifted and settled and cracked."

As Tom Craig returned to the car, Jo sat down with the knapsack on her lap and unfastened the top flap.

"Now—" Granty eased herself into her chair. "What I wished to say this morning, and couldn't, my dear Joanna, was that you *must* leave Winterbloom on Sunday and stay away for good. I spoke with your grandmama yesterday to arrange it. You mustn't end up coming back to be the next 'Miss Ellen Macallan,' trapped here 'til she finally withers away to a ghost. She may be a wicked, selfish creature, but she can make us love her."

"I know," Jo said. "She needed you to keep her safe, but I don't think it's why she wanted me. She said I wasn't to tell you, but I think I have to. She asked me to take this"— she drew the heavy parcel from the knapsack and set it on the table— "and return it to the past, where her father would find it."

"I've not seen that before," Granty said. "What is it?"

The Last Puzzle Piece

Jo gave an uneasy look over her shoulder, and then to the sky, where one small cloud hung above the forest to the south. "I don't know. Is it true she's always been afraid to go through the moon window?"

"Because she saw only flames?" Granty nodded slowly. "Yes, I do believe that. She has always been frightened of fire. She won't have even the electric candles on the table by her bed."

"Then whatever this is, it's been with her all along. It doesn't belong in the past now. It probably couldn't hurt to take it back," Jo said uncertainly, "but I was afraid." She shivered, but it was more from the chill breeze that had sprung up with the dark clouds that had appeared out of nowhere and were racing toward the sun.

Granty pulled nervously at the rings on her fingers. "I think we must open it," she said after a moment. "Promises should be kept, but to make you promise, she told you a truth she knew you would misunderstand."

She reached for the scissors Mrs. Craig had tucked in with a bunch of grapes, for snipping off portions. However, the stitches that bound the heather-colored wool around the stone box were so many and so fine that neither her unsteady fingers nor Jo's sure, stronger ones could find and snip enough to loosen the cover. They were so absorbed in trying that they ignored the wind that whipped around them and snatched the napkins from the table. "Cut the wool,"

Granty said at last. "We can mend it with yarn if need be."

Jo made a cut around three sides of the parcel, and pulled back the top flap like a lid.

The green stone box inside was wrapped around and around with strong waxed cord. The reason for the cord was clear when it was cut and the box fell apart. Both box and lid had been carved from a single piece of bright green, patterned travertine, and they had shattered along the lines of those patterns. Jo picked up a piece of the lid, and Granty another. The designs that covered them looked in some places like the scrap of strange writing on the moon window, but much of their surface was blackened. Granty rubbed her fingers clean on a napkin. "Soot," she said. "But what on earth is *that?*" She pointed to the dark, uneven sphere a little larger than a woman's fist that lay amid the green shards. Black, with here and there a sheen of purple and dark indigo blue, it had a sur-face both irregular and glossily smooth.

Jo reached out a hand to pick it up, and found she could not.

"Hoo, *that's* why the box was so heavy!" she exclaimed. With both hands she managed to lift it and turn it over, to set it down again with a thump on the table. "I don't understand. What is it?"

Granty put up a hand to brush back a blowing lock of hair. "I don't know," she said, looking up, but her eyes were drawn back to the gleaming surface tilted toward her. Suddenly she leaned closer, then gave a little gasp of surprise and beckoned Jo to her side.

"Just there— what do you see?"

"It moved!" Jo exclaimed, and as she stared, the surface seemed to stir again, like mist behind a window.

"It must be a— a seeing stone," Granty said slowly. Behind her, a real mist moved across the ancient clearing, and the wind piled clouds into dark heaps, but neither she nor Jo saw.

"Like a crystal ball, you mean?" Jo asked doubtfully as the first drops of rain fell.

"Like, yes," Granty answered, "but much older."

She bent closer. In the shadow of their two heads the reflection of the clouded sky vanished from the stone's dark circle, and in its place shadows stirred within the stone itself.

"Miss Mac!" Tom Craig's call rang out from among the trees. "Car's O.K.! Don't you rush. I'll bring the umbrellas."

Jo and Granty for the first time looked up and saw the black clouds heaped high to the south, over Winterbloom, and the first rain driving up out of the forest.

Granty was startled into alarm. "I think we must rush." As Jo took a corner of the picnic tablecloth to wipe a spatter from the small, dark mirror, Granty cupped thin, trembling hands around the stone. She looked at Jo and said, "I hardly know what is safe to ask for."

"For Sunday," Jo said. "To see whether I really go."

Granty closed her eyes, then opened them to stare fixedly into the depths of the stone, but its heart remained dark.

"Perhaps it is like the moon window, and only knows what has been, not what will be," she said. "What shall I—"

"Jamie Russell," came Jo's swift answer.

"Of course. James Russell." Granty's lips curved in a smile as she bent her eyes and mind inward to the stone. "James Russell . . ."

Jo, hovering close, saw the shadows in the glass shift, then slowly take on light and shape: first a man's silhouette on a high wall as ropes and a pulley on a high wooden tripod swung a great squared stone into place beside him. Then as another figure, tall and slender, joined him, the forms and faces grew clearer. There stood gruff, red-haired Jamie, and beside him a red-haired boy, much like him, but with Ellen's dark eyebrows, laughing.

"Miss Mac," Young Tom called as he came running up to cover her with a large black umbrella, "you're going to catch your death of pneumonia, and Mother'll say it's my fault." He grinned, then caught a glimpse of the stone as Granty's hand moved up to cover it.

The Last Puzzle Piece

"What's that there? Looks like—" He reached out to heft it in his hand. "Feels like it, too. Meteorite. A 'shooting star' plunk out of the sky. Solid iron. You find it out here?" In his interest he forgot the rain, which had begun to fall heavily.

Granty was suddenly brisk. "No, it's been in the family for ages: our bad-luck piece, you might say. Tom, if you will scoop up this poor picnic and the basket, and then come back for the table and chairs, I have something to show Jo as we come along." She took the umbrella from him, then lifted the stone as casually as if it were ordinary rock. "No, you keep that one," she said as he unfurled a second umbrella and offered it to Jo. "We two will walk together."

"*Bad* luck?" Jo said as Young Tom went trotting back to the car. "How can a shooting star be bad luck?" She held out the knapsack and Granty slipped the stone in.

"Think! Ellen asked you to return it to her father before the fire." The old lady took Jo's elbow and, umbrella in hand, stepped out across the doorstone of the old foundation and veered off into the high, wet grass. "And what would *he* do?"

"Look in it?" Jo said breathlessly. "But could he? I mean, before the fire he still— he already had it in the turret room, in its green box. There couldn't be two of it at once."

"Ellen seemed to think there could, or that the past

163

and present stone would become one." Granty brushed the thought aside. "And yes, he would look into it. And he would see his future in the past that it holds now. *His* future. The fire— that's the danger. Knowing it was to come, he would know how to avoid it or escape or prevent it. Ellen's life would change. Nothing would happen as it has happened, and—"

Thunder rolled along the hill.

"No Russells!" Jo gasped. "No *us*." She stumbled as they reached a large circle of half-buried stone and Granty stopped. "That's what would happen, isn't it? No *any* of us."

"Yes." Granty had almost to shout over the noise of the wind and rain. "Can you pull that clump of weeds out of the center of the stone? No more time for talk."

Baffled, but willing, Jo tugged at the slippery clump, and when it came free was even more puzzled as Granty poked her walking stick down into the hole the weeds had covered. "What is this?" she shouted.

"An old millstone. The hole was for the axle it turned on. The stone was brought up here to cap the old bog-water well. We have no way to destroy your 'shooting star,' but we can put it out of Ellen's reach. There, the hole is clear. Drop the stone in!"

Jo felt the wind beat at her as she drew the stone from the knapsack. The storm swirled into her mind, and she wavered. *To throw a shooting star away . . . when it could tell you so many things . . . show you . . .*

The Last Puzzle Piece

"Jo?"

"I'm all right." Jo knelt on the millstone and reached out to drop the seeing stone through the square hole. For a moment it seemed to her as if the stone refused to leave her hand, but then it dropped down into darkness.

And the wind fell.

"I'll see tomorrow about having the well filled in. With concrete," Granty said breathlessly. "Now come." Young Tom was running toward them through the slackening rain.

"Miss Mac," he said when he reached her side, "I don't care how you squawk, I'm goin' to carry you. Sometimes you don't have the sense God give chickens."

The big old car was within sight of the Winterbloom lane turnoff when Tom Craig's cellular phone gave a shrill buzz. He slowed the car to fish in his pocket for the phone, answered, and listened with a frown.

"We're almost there," he said. "I'll tell Miss Mac."

Granty leaned forward. "Tell me what, Tom?"

He spun the steering wheel in a skidding turn into the Winterbloom lane.

"The house," he said. "Winterbloom House. It's on fire."

Full Circle

The fire burned for hours, and until midafternoon so fiercely that fire engines and tanker trucks came from six nearby towns, including two from across the river in Vermont. Mrs. Craig had been on her way home for the afternoon when she saw smoke pouring from the attic windows, and phoned in the alarm. Because the house was so tall and their ladders too short, after their hurried search of the three lower floors there was little the firemen could do but make sure that sparks and burning embers did not light other fires. After the roof fell in and windows on the third floor broke, they could get water on the flames, but even with an auxiliary pump set up at an old well by the barn, and tanker trucks shuttling back and forth to refill at the Walpole Reservoir, it was never enough. The interior construction of the house was all of heavy oak posts and beams, so it soon was like a charcoal fire built in a tall stone kettle. Only when the stones of the turret toppled into the back garden and the weakened wall above the windows of the Great Hall caved in, were the firefighters able to bring the blaze under control.

Jo found a garden ladder and took a basket with her share of the picnic lunch up to the roof of the low barn, from where she could see almost everything. Granty, damp-haired but dry in one of Mrs. Craig's house dresses, sat down at Mrs. Craig's kitchen table to a small helping of crab salad and half a buttered roll, then allowed herself to be tucked between clean sheets on Young Tom's bed for the rest of the afternoon. Mrs. Craig served iced tea and coffee and cookies to firemen until suppertime, and then called Jo and Thomas and Young Tom in for a meal of roast chicken, apple salad, and crumb cake. Afterward, Thomas and Young Tom went back to their garden hoses and the fire. They took with them two garden chairs to set up on the grass near the front gate, safely away from any wall that might topple, for Granty and Jo.

"Safer out here if any more wall topples down," Old Thomas explained. It was the first time Jo had heard him say a word.

Jo and Granty had not been alone together since

the first confusion of the fire. For a while, as dusk gathered in the forest and under the orchard trees, they watched the spiraling smoke, and the hot spots that flared up from time to time behind the gaping windows.

"They say it started in the turret. But how could it?" Jo asked at last. "Even if Ellen got up there and saw the flames and opened the window on them, fire couldn't come in from the past."

"Who knows what she had the power to do?" was Granty's slow answer. "She lost her last chance to erase the past. Anger and despair could have made her strong enough for anything. At least no one else was hurt."

As she spoke, a car sped through the gate and braked sharply as it turned onto the grass across the drive. The door opened and a figure ran toward them. It was Mrs. Lucas.

"Grandma!" Jo jumped up to throw her arms around her.

"Peggy, dear!" Granty was surprised and bewildered. "Where did you come from? How did you hear?"

Mrs. Lucas bent to kiss her. "Your Mrs. Craig phoned Colorado right after she called the fire department and her son, and our dog-sitter reached me at our hotel in Los Angeles. I left for the airport without a stitch of luggage, and caught the next flight out. I'm afraid I broke the speed limit most of the way up from the Boston airport."

Jo hugged her again. "It's great. But why?"

"To take both of you back to Colorado, of course."

"Oh, no, Peggy." Granty shook her head. "I shall be happy to leave, but Colorado is in the wrong direction."

"Where then? To Cousin Susan's?" Mrs. Lucas asked. "You don't mean back to New York, do you? It's another world from the New York you left all those years ago."

"No, New York is my past," Granty said firmly. "I've no time to waste on the past. We will look in the Yellow Pages for somewhere to stay until the weekend. You will ask Henry to join us when his conference is over, and the four of us will sail for Europe. Or fly. Since my jigsaw puzzle has burned to ash, I have a mind to see the towers of Carcassonne for myself."

Jo's eyes widened. "Granty! Really?"

At that moment, Tom Craig came around the side of the house, dragging a heavy object through the grass, using a pickax as hook. "Miss Mac," he said as he came up, "looks like this here's about the only thing except the stone walls that didn't burn up or melt down. Found it in the orchard. Glass is gone, but under the soot, it's fine."

Mrs. Lucas clapped her hands. "Oh, it's that beautiful old attic window!"

Granty's smile was grim. "If it's cool now, Tom, please lock it up in the barn. Tomorrow you can take a hacksaw to it and cut it into pieces. When I sail to France I shall drop them all safely overboard."

"If you say so, Miss Mac." Tom headed toward the barn, shaking his head.

Mrs. Lucas was just as puzzled. "But Granty—why?"

"It's a long story," Jo said.

"A long and sad one," old Miss Macallan added. "And you won't believe a word of it."

"Oh, I don't know. Does it have anything to do with Witch Ellen?" Mrs. Lucas asked unexpectedly. "I might surprise you."

The three of them smiled at each other in wonder and turned for a moment to watch the centuries-old fire burn to ash at last.